THE FLIGHT OF DRAGONS

The Fourth Tale from
THE FIVE KINGDOMS

THE
FLIGHT OF DRAGONS

VIVIAN FRENCH

ILLUSTRATED BY ROSS COLLINS

CANDLEWICK PRESS

Text copyright © 2010 by Vivian French
Illustrations copyright © 2010 by Ross Collins

First U. S. edition 2011

Library of Congress Cataloging-in-Publication Data

French, Vivian.
The flight of dragons : the fourth tale from the five kingdoms /
Vivian French ; [illustrations by Ross Collins]. — 1st U.S. ed.
p.   cm.
(Tales from the five kingdoms)
Summary: On Gracie Gillypot's birthday, greedy, chocolate-hungry twins
awaken the banished Old Malignant One, and unless Gracie can find
a powerful, long-forgotten dragon's egg, the Five Kingdoms
may succumb to evil magic and Total Oblivion.
ISBN 978-0-7636-5083-4
[1. Fairy tales.] — I. Collins, Ross, ill. II. Title. III. Series.
PZ8.F897Fli 2011
[Fic] — dc22   2010040130

11 12 13 14 15 16 BVG 10 9 8 7 6 5 4 3 2 1

Printed in Berryville, VA, U.S.A.

This book was typeset in Baskerville.

Candlewick Press
99 Dover Street
Somerville, Massachusetts 02144

visit us at www.candlewick.com

For Mike Dixon and Lorna Renshaw,
and all the team working in the Breast Cancer Unit
at the Western General Hospital, Edinburgh,
with admiration, love, and gratitude

Boo! to the Old Malignancy!

PRINCIPAL CHARACTERS

Prince Marcus	second in line to the throne of Gorebreath
Gracie Gillypot	a Trueheart
Gubble	a domesticated troll
Professor Scallio	former tutor to Prince Marcus
Marlon	a bat
Millie	Marlon's daughter
Samson	an extremely small bat, no relation to Marlon, and not very important
Alf	Marlon's nephew
Great-Uncle Alvin	Marlon's great-uncle
Queen Bluebell	Queen of Wadingburn
King Horace	King of Niven's Knowe
Princess Fedora	oldest daughter of Kesta, Queen of Dreghorn; married to Prince Tertius
Prince Tertius	only son of King Horace
Bobby	page in the palace of Niven's Knowe
Saturday Mousewater	housemaid in the palace of Niven's Knowe
Marshling Stonecrop	a boy
Thistly Canker	longtime resident in Niven's Knowe
Conducta Canker	Thistly's daughter
Globula Canker	Conducta's twin
Great Grandpa Canker	also known as Old Malignancy, aka Mercy Grinder, a seriously evil character banished to live beyond the borders of the Five Kingdoms
Carrion Crow	a crow; a spy for Old Malignancy

DRAGONS
Lumiere • Indigo • Luskentyre

THE ANCIENT CRONES

Edna	the Ancient One
Elsie	the Oldest
Val	the Youngest
Foyce	Gracie's stepsister and apprentice crone

Chapter One

"Dragons?" Professor Scallio peered over the top of his spectacles. "MORE dragons? Where were they this time?"

The very young bat perched on a shelf in the ancient library of Wadingburn Palace opened his mouth, but no sound came out. A much older bat, balanced precariously on a pile of books on the professor's desk, gave him a sharp look. "Give us the gossip, kiddo. Quick smart! No time to hang about!"

The very young bat began to quiver. "If you please, Mr. Marlon Batster," he whispered. "I ain't accustomed to human people."

Marlon gave a snort of disapproval. "Thought you wanted to learn the biz."

"Oh, I do, Mr. Marlon Batster! I do!" The little bat flapped his wings. "When you said I could be a Batster

Super Spotter, I was so excited, I was all of a flap, so to speak, but I didn't know you'd want me to talk to human people." He gave the professor a nervous glance. "They're SCARY!"

"Not as scary as I'll be if you don't spill the beans, young Samson," Marlon said cheerfully. "Come on, kid. You can do it. How many dragons? Where? What time?"

Samson screwed up his eyes and took a deep breath. "Three of them. One gold, one blue, and one green. Beyond the southern border. Twilight yesterday."

"That's more like it," Marlon told him. "Now hop to. You know the drill. Any more sightings and you're back here, pronto."

"Yes, Mr. Marlon Batster, sir. Certainly, Mr. Batster, sir. Erm . . . Mr. Batster?"

Marlon lifted an imperious claw. "Spit it out, kid."

"Ma said I had to go straight back to bed, Mr. Marlon Batster, sir."

Marlon sighed. "Can't get quality help these days. OK, young Samson. Scoot." Samson scooted, and Marlon turned to Professor Scallio. "So. What d'you make of that?"

The professor shook his head and picked up a piece of paper from his desk. "That's the fourth time your spotters have seen dragons in the South. There's one report from the North, two from the West, and so far nothing definite from this side of the Five Kingdoms, although Millie heard a farm boy telling his friends he'd seen a dragon. Luckily he'd spent most of the afternoon in the Pig Catcher's Tavern, so nobody believed him."

"Good girl, my Millie." Marlon allowed himself a fond smile. "Not much gets past her."

Professor Scallio stroked his chin. "So far the dragons have been seen only at daybreak and twilight, and they're flying well outside the borders and keeping away from humans. But there's something going on . . . and it's worrisome. Very worrisome. What could they want?"

Before Marlon could answer, the library door flew open. Prince Marcus, second in line to the throne of Gorebreath, came striding in, his hair standing on end and his riding jacket covered in mud. "Hi, Prof!" he said. "Nina-Rose is staying at our place, and I can't stand it any longer, so I came to see you. Arry's behaving like a dying duck in a thunderstorm, and Father keeps talking about 'jolly little lovebirds, ho-ho-ho!' and Mother's flapping around like a headless chicken. It's murder. I was going to go and see Gracie, but

Mother wants me at home tonight for a hideous family dinner, so I'm going tomorrow instead. It's Gracie's birthday soon, by the way. Thought I'd take her on an adventure—but I don't know where yet. Oh! Hello, Marlon! Didn't see you there!"

"Hi, kiddo."

Marlon didn't sound his usual chirpy self, and Marcus swung around to inspect him. "What's up? You and the prof plotting something?"

The professor and the bat exchanged self-conscious glances, and Marcus brightened visibly. "You *are*! What is it?" He looked at the pile of books on the desk, and his eyes grew wide. "*Dragons: An Introduction. The Larger Beasts of the Five Kingdoms—with pencil illustrations. Illnesses, Abscesses, and Heat Complaints with Reference to Dragons and Other Scaled Beasts.* Wow! Have you found one? A dragon?"

"Certainly not." Professor Scallio folded his arms. "Nothing of the kind. I . . . I was just doing some research. On dragons. Wasn't I, Marlon?"

"Sure thing, Prof. Research 'n' all that stuff," Marlon agreed.

Marcus had opened one of the books and was flicking through the pages. "Hey," he said, "look at this! It's Niven's Knowe—there's a drawing of a whole load of dragons outside Terty's palace! How come?"

A pained expression crossed the professor's face. "A flight of dragons, dear boy. A flight."

"A what?" Marcus looked blank.

His old tutor clicked his tongue disapprovingly. "Really, Marcus. Didn't I teach you anything? Collective noun. Herd of cows. Flock of geese. Flight of dragons."

Marlon waved a claw. "Colony of bats."

"Cloud of bats," squeaked a fourth voice from high up among the bookshelves. "Ma always said it was a cloud of bats."

"Alf?" Marlon, the professor, and Marcus squinted up into the darkness. "Is that you?"

There was a flurry of small black wings, and Alf appeared, blinking in the light. "Howdy, Unc. Hi, Mr. Prince. Morning, Professor." He yawned and stretched. "I was asleep. Up all last night on the western border. Somebody seen more dragons?"

"I knew something was going on!" Marcus beamed. "A flight of dragons . . . doesn't that sound good? Brilliant, in fact." A thought struck him, and his smile grew wider. "Wouldn't that be the best-ever birthday present for Gracie? An adventure where she sees a flight of dragons!" He turned over another page. "Look, Alf. Aren't they amazing? Shame they're not in color. Oh! There's the archway at the back of Terty's place. Even that's got dragons carved on it. But why are they there? Terty'd have a purple fit if a dragon came anywhere near him."

Alf began to snigger, but a warning glare from his uncle silenced him. Professor Scallio put the tips of his fingers together and considered his reply. The kings and queens of the Five Kingdoms had never encouraged their offspring to study the past; it was considered much safer to enjoy the present and look to the future. The professor's view was that an understanding of past events might prevent the repetition of mistakes; King Frank — father of Marcus and his twin brother, Arioso — had always disagreed. "It'll just give 'em ideas!" he had boomed. "Especially Marcus! The boy's got far too many ideas as it is! Dangerous things, ideas."

Marcus looked up from the book and guessed the professor's dilemma. "It's OK," he said with a grin. "You're not my tutor anymore. Were there really dragons at Niven's Knowe? Or is it just a story?"

"Indeed, there were." The professor sat back and waited for the onslaught of questions.

"WOW! When? Why did they go away? Who got rid of them?" Marcus was on his feet and wild to hear more. "Will they ever come back? What—"

"Hang on, kiddo!" Marlon raised a wing in warning. "Here comes Her Majesty! Company with her, by the sound of it, so I'll be offski. Back soon as. See ya!" And he was gone before Professor Scallio could stop him.

Alf flew hastily back to the darkness and settled down to watch.

Marcus, in an agony of suspense, waited as the door opened and Bluebell, Queen of Wadingburn, came sailing in. Behind her puffed a well-rounded gentleman who was protesting, "Pretty young thing's doing her best, Bluebell, m'dear. Sure of it. Just need to get it sorted out."

"You certainly do! Can't imagine coping without a cook. Whatever was Fedora thinkin' of? Oh!" The queen's eye fell on Marcus, and her expression changed from irritation to pleasure. "Dear boy! How nice to see you!"

Marcus was looking at Bluebell's companion, his face alight. "King Horace! Sire! I've just discovered something absolutely amazing. You used to keep dragons at Niven's Knowe!"

"What?" The king turned a curious shade of purple. "Certainly not! Not in my lifetime. As if I'd allow such a thing! Whole idea is ridiculous — totally ridiculous. Never heard of anything so stupid. Luckily my grandfather was a man of sense. Said no king could call himself civilized when he had dragons rampaging around his kingdom; never believed those silly superstitions about evil coming in if the dragons went out. Got rid of the lot of them eighty years ago — and not a moment too soon. And not a sign of evil! Not a sign!"

"Oh." Marcus did his best to hide his disappointment. "I wouldn't mind having a few dragons in Gorebreath."

Up in his lofty perch, Alf applauded enthusiastically, but Queen Bluebell peered over her lorgnette. "Don't be silly, Marcus. There'd be young women screaming all over the place — and think of the cost! You can't feed a dragon on peanuts, you know. And there'd be endless fire damage to pay for — you can't keep dragons caged up, so they'd have to be taken for walks and so on, and there'd be accidents with haystacks and thatched cottages and wooden sheds for sure. Besides, there are laws about that sort of thing. 'No Undesirable and Non-Permitted Residents,' if I remember rightly. No zombies, sorceresses, werewolves, or unreliable creatures of any kind allowed in the Five Kingdoms, and that includes dragons. Exclusion Laws, that's what they're called. Keep us safe in our beds at night."

King Horace was still glaring at Marcus. "Ancient history, those dragons. Where'd you find out about 'em?"

Marcus, taken aback by the king's reaction, pointed to the open book. "It's all in there, sire. There are pictures of them outside your palace."

"What? What, what, WHAT?" The king gave every appearance of being about to explode. "Thought those books had all been destroyed! Never allow rubbish like that in my library. Look to the future, that's my motto. What's past is past, and best left that way. I'm shocked, Bluebell, shocked to the core! Thought you'd have known better."

Bluebell raised her lorgnette and inspected the page. "Don't see the harm in a little history, myself. Hmph! Fancy that! Dragons carved on the archway. Don't remember ever seeing those."

"I can assure you, Bluebell, m'dear, that those are long, long gone! Cut them out years ago!" The king was still trembling with anger as he leaned across the table and slammed the book shut. He gave the professor a cold stare. "I'd suggest you burn these books before they cause trouble. History! Stuff and nonsense, the whole lot of it! Now, I must be off. Promised young Tertius I'd be home for tea. If there is any, that is." His frown deepened. "If you should hear of a reasonable sort of cook, Bluebell, old girl, send us a pigeon with a message."

Bluebell slapped her forehead. "Knew we'd come here for a reason. Be a good chap, Professor, and ask your sister to put the word out. The palace of Niven's Knowe needs a cook; Princess Fedora's sent the old one packing." She turned back to the king. "If I find a suitable candidate, Horace, I'll bring her to Niven's Knowe myself. If your son's foolish enough to allow his brand-new wife to upset one of the best cooks in the Five Kingdoms, he deserves every dried-up kipper he gets, and it's time somebody told him a few home truths!"

Alf started to giggle, wobbled, slipped—and only just saved himself from falling into view. Made wary by his narrow escape, he moved farther into the darkness, and settled himself on a dusty pile of papers. His eyelids began to droop; only the boom of King Horace's voice kept him awake.

"Now, now." The king's belligerent expression melted into a sentimental smile. "Fedora's a pretty little thing, and I'm sure she means well. It'll be teething troubles,

that's all. Expect it'll settle down in a day or two."
King Horace nodded wisely, and puffed his way out
of the library.

"Hmph!" Bluebell shook her head. " 'Pretty little
thing,' indeed! Fedora needs a good shake, if you ask
me. Still, not my place. I'd better be off. Good to see
you, Marcus. Bring that nice girl Gracie Gillypot with
you next time." With a cheery wave, she sailed out of
the library.

Professor Scallio watched her go, then turned to
look out the window, his brow furrowed.

Marcus sat down on the edge of the desk. "I can't
believe the laws won't allow dragons into the Five
Kingdoms. No wonder the place is so boring."

His old tutor gave a noncommittal grunt. "Did you
say you were going to see Gracie tomorrow?"

Marcus nodded. "Yes. I'll go as early as I can, or
Nina-Rose'll try and make me join her and Arry on
some ghastly outing to make daisy chains or pick roses
or skip among the dewdrops."

All but asleep, Alf chuckled to himself. A moment
later, he was snoring steadily, his effort to stay awake
abandoned.

"Hmm . . ." The professor was still staring out at the
clouds, an abstracted expression on his face. "I wonder.

Marcus, could you do me a favor? Ask my sister, Val, if she's noticed anything odd about the web of power."

"The web?" Marcus was immediately curious. "Am I allowed to ask why, sir?"

"No." Professor Scallio sounded irritable, but as Marcus looked at him in surprise, he went on, "I'm sorry, dear boy. You'll have to excuse me. There's something on my mind. Just do as I ask—there's a good lad. I'll see you again soon." And the old man sat down and pulled a pile of books toward him.

Marcus hesitated. Then he said, "You can trust me, sir. I'm not a kid anymore. If there's something wrong, I might be able to help. Me and Gracie, that is . . ."

There was a pause before the professor looked up. He studied his former pupil with some care, while Marcus did his best to be patient. "I *do* trust you, Marcus," he said at last. "And Gracie. And you may well be able to help, you and Gracie and the Ancient Crones." He glanced toward the library door and lowered his voice. "There have been sightings of dragons, and no dragon has been seen near the borders of the Five Kingdoms for decades. Marlon's been keeping watch for me, he and his team of bats. So far no humans have seen them, but it's only a matter of time—and then there'll be total panic, and the armies will be called out, and who knows what'll happen then? Dragons are incredibly powerful beasts; they make excellent friends but very terrible enemies. Very terrible, indeed."

"I see." Marcus was trying hard not to bubble over with excitement. "I'll tell Gracie, and I'll ask the crones if they know anything."

"Excellent. But Marcus . . . remember. Not a word to anyone else!"

Marcus stood at attention and saluted. "You have the word of Prince Marcus of Gorebreath, sir!" He grinned, leaned forward, and slapped the professor on the back. "But you have to admit, Prof—it is REALLY exciting!" And he strode out of the library, whistling as he went.

A moment later, he was back, still grinning. "Hey! Do you think they're trying to get back to Niven's Knowe? That'd give old Terty a scare and a half!" And he was off again, leaving the professor looking extremely thoughtful.

Chapter Two

Back in the kingdom of Niven's Knowe, the pretty little thing was throwing a tantrum. It was her third that day, and her husband, Prince Tertius, was doing his best to soothe her.

"Darling Fedora, I *promise* we'll find another cook soon. Father's gone to ask Queen Bluebell if she knows of one, and very soon you'll be able to have your breakfast eggies exactly the way you like them. And your fishy pie. And chocolate cake with chocolate-cream icing three times a day if that's what you want."

Fedora pouted. "But you promised that yesterday, Terty, *and* the day before. And I'm TIRED of rubbery eggs and bony pies, and we haven't had chocolate cake for ages and ages and *ages.* Your head butler's a simply dreadful cook, and if my dinners don't get better soon, I'm going home to Mother."

Tertius went pale. "Oh, dearest darling BEAUTIFUL Fedora—please don't say that!" He hesitated. "We could . . . we could ask Mrs. Basket if she'd come back." Fedora's face darkened, and he went on quickly. "I know you hate her, and you told her you never ever wanted to see her again, but she *is* a very good cook. And she's been here more than thirty years, and she's still in her cottage, and it's only just across the park, and I could ask her to make you the loveliest chocolate cake you've ever seen. She's sure to do it if I ask her, because she's known me since I was a baby, and she's a big old softie if you get on the right side of her."

"NO!" His bride scowled. "She said I was the fussiest eater she'd ever met. All I did was tell her I don't like brussels sprouts. Or cabbage. Or smelly kippers. Or lumpy custard—"

Tertius could bear it no longer. "Hang on a minute! Mrs. Basket makes the best custard ever!"

"I didn't say she didn't," Fedora said petulantly. "I was just trying to be 'observant of the kitchen and what goes on there,' like it says in *The Handbook of Palace Management* that Great-Aunt Gussie gave me as a wedding present. The next bit says, 'Always inform Cook of your desires and wishes in a firm but kindly manner,' so that was what I was doing. And then she went all huffy and said she'd never had any complaints before, so I said there was a first time for everything, and that was when she asked if you knew I'd come to see her and I said no. And then she sniffed and said she'd always thought you'd end up with a bossy young thing for a wife. She was rude to me, Terty, and I'm not having her in my palace!"

There was a brief silence while Tertius wondered what would happen if he pointed out that it was a long way from being Fedora's palace. His father, King Horace, was very much alive and active; indeed, at this precise moment, he was doing his best to make his daughter-in-law happy in her new home by finding a new palace cook. Deciding to play it safe, Tertius said, "Well. Let's wait and see what Father says. Shall we go and play spillikins, darling one?"

Fedora shrugged. "If you want. But I won't feel better unless I have some chocolate."

"Dearest — I'll send for a page this minute." The prince tugged at a velvet bellpull, and there was a resounding *clang! clang! clang!* somewhere deep down below.

In the servants' quarters, three tall footmen, four middle-size housemaids, and five small pages leaped to their feet, but the head butler waved them back to their seats around the kitchen table with an imperious gesture.

"Nobody leaves this kitchen until we're in agreement," he boomed. "A stand has to be taken! Mrs. Basket was dismissed for no good reason. Thirty-five years she's been here, and never a word against her or her cooking until that spoiled little madam arrived."

There were nods and mutters and murmurs of "You never said a truer word, Mr. Trout."

Mr. Trout nodded. "So—are we all agreed? Until Mrs. Basket is returned to her post, we're on strike. No more answering of bells. No more cleaning or mopping or serving the meals. And"—he banged the table with a heavy iron ladle—"NO COOKING!"

The youngest of the housemaids giggled nervously. "But what about *our* dinners, Mr. Trout, sir?"

The head butler gave her a look that made her blush a deep crimson and wish she had never spoken. "Naturally we will look after ourselves," he said stiffly.

One of the footmen cleared his throat. "Ahem. Are we to presume you will be informing Prince Tertius of the state of affairs?"

"Of course." Mr. Trout put the iron ladle down and adjusted his tailcoat. "I shall take the opportunity offered by the ringing of that there bell to announce the situation to the young prince this very minute."

The smallest page wriggled uncomfortably on his

chair. "'Scuse me for mentioning it, sir, but what about King Horace? He's ever so kind and nice, and he does like his hot buttered toast and tea at five o'clock. 'Bobby,' he says to me, every single day, 'Bobby, toast is one of the finest things a man can have.' And he always cuts off the crusts, seeing as his teeth ain't what they were, and he lets me have them with ever such a lot of butter on them."

Mr. Trout directed his look at the smallest page — but it had little effect. Bobby was lost in a dream of buttered toast crusts.

"The lad's got a point, Mr. Trout, sir," one of the footmen ventured. "The old king didn't want Mrs. Basket to go. I heard him pleading with Princess Fedora, but she wouldn't listen."

Mr. Trout stroked his chin thoughtfully, then nodded. "Fair enough. Tea and toast for His Majesty, but that's the end of it. And that's —"

He was interrupted by the bell in the corner of the kitchen jerking into action, and his words were lost in the urgent *clang! clang! clang!* of a second summons.

"I'll be on my way," he said grimly, and left the kitchen with a heavy and purposeful tread.

Chapter Three

The House of the Ancient Crones lay hidden in a hollow on the fringes of the Less Enchanted Forest, protected from prying eyes by a thick green mist. Gracie Gillypot, who was a Trueheart, was aware of the mist but could easily see through it; strangers hoping to visit the house found this mist to be an impenetrable fog. They inevitably got lost and walked around and around in ever-decreasing circles until rescued. The crones were elderly and had no desire to leave the comfort of their warm rooms unless it was absolutely necessary; it was much easier to ask Gracie to run outside to check on any visitors—either Gracie or Gubble. Gubble, however, was less reliable. He was a squat green troll with firm ideas. If he didn't like the look of an incomer, he was inclined to leave them to their own panic-stricken devices while he stomped back home, humming tunelessly. Sometimes this was unfortunate; the crones boosted their income by weaving cloth of the highest quality on their second loom, and messengers who had already endured the dangers of the long journey from the Five Kingdoms did not take kindly to this extra peril and demanded lower prices in recompense.

"We're going to have to sort this out," the Oldest One told Gracie. She was sitting at the kitchen table surrounded by pieces of paper, and her sums were not adding up. "It was so much better when Marlon organized our orders for us."

"Rubbish, Elsie." The Ancient One had popped in to WATER WINGS to make herself a cup of tea. "Your mind's failing. It was a nightmare. Marlon was always doing special deals without asking us, and it lost us a fortune. Don't you remember the black velvet dress we made for Lady Lamorna? She practically got it at cost. That bat has a lot to answer for!"

Elsie took off her wig of tumbling red curls, scratched her bald head, and put the wig back on. "I suppose so," she said, "but all the dresses we made for Princess Fedora's wedding had to be reduced in price because Gubble led Queen Kesta's messenger into the

Unwilling Bushes and never mentioned it until the following morning."

Gracie hid a smile. "The messenger did call Gubble a lot of nasty names when he first met him, Auntie Elsie. And the next time he came, he was *very* polite."

Elsie sighed. "I don't suppose we could lift the mist, could we?"

The Ancient One looked appalled, and her one blue eye flashed. "Elsie! The very idea! We're not here just to supply the people of the Five Kingdoms with dresses and robes, you know. We're here to keep them safe. If the web of power had no protection, all kinds of dreadful things might happen. There are forces of evil and wickedness just biding their time out there . . . waiting for the moment when the web breaks to wreak havoc in every way they can. Don't EVER let me hear you mention such a thing again!" She picked up her cup and sailed out of the kitchen.

"I know, I know." There were tears in Elsie's eyes as she went back to her bills. "I really do. But sometimes I think things would be so much easier if it wasn't all so terribly mysterious and magical. If only people could just come and knock on the door, collect their parcels, and leave again."

Gracie leaned across the table and patted her hand.

"Auntie Edna didn't mean to be cross," she said. "She's worried about something. She snapped at Auntie Val earlier for not working hard enough, and she was furious with Foyce when she muddled up the threads. I think the web isn't flowing as smoothly as it usually does, and she doesn't know why."

Elsie gave Gracie's hand a squeeze. "What did we ever do without you, dear? It's been a different place since you came to live here. How that dreadful step-father of yours could have treated you the way he did I just cannot understand." She shook her head with one careful hand on her wig to keep it in place. "It only goes to show how wicked he must have been. He and Foyce. Why, when you came here, you brought the sunshine with you." Elsie gave a sentimental sniff before taking out a large handkerchief and blowing her nose. "And I'm sure you're right about Edna and the web. There's a roughness on the surface; I noticed it yesterday, and it's not getting any better." Elsie shook her head. "I'll just get on with my adding up and try not to be a silly old woman."

"Why don't I make us some tea," Gracie suggested. "And there might be some cookies, if Gubble hasn't taken them all —"

"UG!" A cupboard door opened, and an outraged

figure peered out. "UG! Gubble not take cookies! Gubble EAT cookies!"

Gracie smiled and went to put the kettle on.

Gubble, after a couple of failed attempts, installed himself on a stool next to Elsie. "Gubble help," he announced. Picking up a card of thread samples, he ate it with an expression of martyred duty.

"The most helpful thing you could do, Gubble," Elsie told him as she hastily removed the more important orders, "is show visitors the right way to the front door and *not* leave them up to their necks in mud."

"Maybe Gubble and I could have a little practice tomorrow?" Gracie put a plate of bread and butter on the table. "Unless you want me to work on the looms, that is."

Elsie shook her head. "Val's coming in early, and Foyce is beginning to be much more reliable. You take Gubble out for the day. It'll do you both good to get some fresh air. And you never know; you might meet that nice young man of yours."

Gracie turned a startling shade of pink. "I've told you, Auntie Elsie. We're just good friends."

"And my name's Lillibelle Lackabone," Elsie said, and winked at Gubble. "We know about Prince Marcus, don't we, Gubble?"

Gubble chuckled a deep chuckle. "Prince like Gracie. Gracie like Prince. Hand-holding and—"

"If you don't want any bread and butter, Gubble," Gracie interrupted, "I'll take it away."

With an effort, Gubble wrenched his mind toward the needs of his large green stomach. "Want bread. Jam, please."

Elsie got up and fetched the jam from a cupboard. "There you are. And tomorrow morning, I'll make you a nice picnic, with enough for three."

Gracie blushed again but said nothing.

Chapter Four

By twelve o'clock the following day, the situation at the palace of Niven's Knowe had taken a distinct turn for the worse. Princess Fedora was sulking, and Prince Tertius was staring at his feet. *The Handbook of Palace Management* was lying abandoned on the floor beside Fedora's chair; every so often Tertius gave it a baleful glare. Thanks to Fedora's passionate belief in the *Handbook*'s words of wisdom, the palace was not only without a cook but also missing a head butler, three footmen, three housemaids, and four pages. Only one of the housemaids—a pale, dutiful girl called Saturday Mousewater—and Bobby, the smallest page, remained.

"I don't know what Father's going to say," Tertius said gloomily. "He'll be back from his walk soon, and he'll be expecting his lunch."

"Is that all you can think about?" Fedora snapped. "What about ME?"

Her young husband shrugged. "I thought you said you were going home to your mother."

Fedora sat up straight. She had, indeed, in the heat of the moment announced her immediate return to the arms of Queen Kesta but on second thought had decided against it. Her sisters would ask too many questions, and there was a faint possibility that her mother might not be entirely sympathetic. Kesta had given her daughter a number of Helpful Hints on a Happy Marriage, and number one had been to throw away Great-Aunt Gussie's gift.

"It's a dreadful book," the queen had said. "The thing is, you must always be terribly, *terribly* nice to servants. They're far more important than visiting royalty. If you can't have a comfortable life with lots of lovely meals and pages to bring you cups of tea when you want them, WHAT is the point of being a queen?" Fedora, however, had been instantly attracted to the steely-eyed monarch gracing the title page of the *Handbook* and had resolved to follow all of its instructions to the letter. She had often thought her mother was much too easy-going; she herself was going to be a model of etiquette and style and the undisputed ruler of all palace affairs.

Tertius's mother had died many years ago; what King Horace and his son undoubtedly needed was a Strong Hand in Charge. (Page 43: "Always make it clear that instant dismissal will follow if your orders are not immediately obeyed; argument, hesitation, or delay will also result in termination of contract. No discussion is to be permitted; this will suggest WEAKNESS, and WEAKNESS has no place in a well-run palace.")

"No, Terty dearest. I've been thinking. All we have to do is put up a notice in the marketplace saying there are one or two vacancies here at the palace." Fedora picked up her *Handbook*. "There's a whole section here about appointing new staff, and of course I'll interview them myself."

Tertius took a deep breath. For a second he considered throwing the book out of the window into the weed-infested moat, but a smile from his beloved—the first for some long time—melted his resolution. "Fedora, darling . . . if that's what you want. You write the notice, and I'll send Bobby."

Fedora gave him another gracious smile. "Thank you, Terty. Now, let me see . . ." She picked up a piece of parchment, complete with a shining royal seal, and sucked the top of her pen. "One cook. Do we really need a head butler?"

"Yes," Tertius said firmly. "Father would be miserable without one. He and Mr. Trout used to play checkers together every night. You'd better add a note about that. Not chess, mind. Father hates chess." He rubbed his nose. "Actually, it might make Father feel better about losing Mrs. Basket if you can find a new head butler who sometimes lets him win. Mr. Trout used to win all the time."

"If you say so, dearest." Fedora blew him a kiss. "And what about six footmen, all the same height? They'd look SO smart! *Much* better than the old ones . . . and a couple of housemaids. That should be enough, don't you think? I'm sure Bobby can manage on his own. And if we don't have any more pages, it'll pay for the extra footmen." The young housekeeper looked pleased with her thoughtful economies. "And we could get an extra coachman . . . AND a new coach." At which point Fedora drifted off into a wonderful dream, where she was driven around the Five Kingdoms in a pink-and-silver coach with her name and coat of arms emblazoned in large gold letters on the door. She was trying to decide whether she should have a matching pink dress or go with a contrast in delicate turquoise, when the door opened and Bobby announced, "Look out, all! Here comes the king, Your — erm — Highnesses."

King Horace came bustling in, his brow furrowed. "Tertius! Whatever's happened? I came home and there was nobody around except that poor little housemaid with big feet. Had to hang up my own coat. Poor soul couldn't reach, although she did try. And Bobby tells me the footmen have gone!"

Tertius looked meaningfully at Fedora, who bristled. "*You* tell him," she whispered. "He's your father!"

"But it was you who got rid of them all!" Tertius hissed back.

Fedora glared at him. "Actually, Father-in-Law," she began, "there's been a bit of a . . . a bit of a change." Seeing King Horace's face, she hastily added, "It'll all be fine — I promise. I've got it all under control. Haven't I, Terty dear?"

Tertius, considerably braver now that his father had come home, shrugged. "If you say so, darling."

"I do. Dearest. Sweetie pie. Poppetty woozle." Fedora turned her back on her beloved as she scribbled furiously. "By this time tomorrow, we'll have a lovely new cook and housemaids, and as soon as they're settled in, I'll sort out the butler and the footmen and the pages, and it'll all be as right as rain. Only lots better. Bobby! Would you run to the marketplace and pin this on the notice board?"

Bobby, who had been hovering in the doorway, dashed forward. "Sure thing, Your Highness. And when I get back, shall I bring King H. some toast? I'm an expert at making toast. Mrs. Basket says—"

"Thank you, Bobby. That's quite enough." Fedora was beginning to feel she was losing control. "Take the notice, and then you can come back and make toast. And tea. In fact, you could make it for all three of us."

King Horace looked shifty. "Actually," he said, "I've already had a little snack. Called in on Mrs. Basket, as I happened to be in that direction, and she just happened to be taking a steak-and-kidney pudding out of the oven. Felt a bit peckish after nothing but cold porridge for breakfast, y'see." Catching sight of Fedora's appalled expression, he felt it might be tactful to change the subject. "Expect you know what you're doing, m'dear." The king fished in his pocket and extracted a shiny silver coin. "Off you go, Bobby, my lad, and buy yourself a pie while you're out."

"Yikes! Thanks very much, King H. I'll be back in a jiffy!" And Bobby sped out of the door, his face one huge happy smile.

Tertius sat down with a *flump*. "You could have asked him to get a pie for me, too, Father. I don't suppose that Mousewater girl is any good at cooking, and Feddy can't even boil an egg. I'm not going to survive for the rest of the day on nothing but toast and tea, I can tell you."

Fedora stood up and marched across the room. "You're an ungrateful pig, Terty, and you don't deserve me. I'm going straight to the kitchen, and I'm going to cook us the most delicious lunch ever. So there!" And she flounced through the door, slamming it hard behind her.

"Dear me . . ." King Horace's eyes were very round. "Is that how girls usually behave?"

Tertius had no time to reply. Fedora had reappeared, her eyes still flashing thunderbolts; she was storming back across the room to collect her *Handbook*. "We'll see," she said through gritted teeth, "what the suggested menu is for Tuesdays. I'll ring the gong when it's ready. Good-*bye!*" And she was gone with another mighty *CRASH!* that left the portraits swinging on the wall in mute protest.

Chapter Five

A mile or so away from the palace of Niven's Knowe, Thistly Canker, arms folded, was glaring at her twin daughters. "I've had enough," she announced. "More than enough. You're big girls now. Far too big to be cluttering up my house, lying around like pigs in a sty and never lifting a finger except when you want to push food into your greedy, grasping mouths. There's nothing I can do with that useless lump you call your father, but I was a Mousewater before I was stupid enough to take up with a Canker, and Mousewaters have always earned an honest wage. Now, you two may be Cankers by name, but you've Mousewater blood in you — so out you go, and don't come back until you've got work. Understand?"

The twins looked at each other. Conducta shrugged, and Globula rolled her eyes. Thistly saw the exchange and picked up a rolling pin. Her daughters heaved themselves to their feet and dragged themselves to the door.

"You'll be sorry for this, Ma," Conducta said grimly as she lifted the old wooden latch.

"*Really* sorry," Globula echoed as she followed her sister out into the lane that led to the market square.

The Canker twins had no heart. Few of the Cankers did; as they were descended from zombie ancestors, this was a family weakness. Or strength, depending on your point of view. Conducta and Globula had no use for such an organ; their beady-eyed observation of other girls had led them to believe the possession of a heart was a distinct disadvantage. All that weeping and wailing about boys. And stupid tears about icky-picky kittens with no whiskers. No. The twins had their dreams, and there was no trace of sentimentality or concern for others to get in their way. The two of them fully intended to get extremely rich as soon as possible and spend the rest of their lives ordering people around and eating chocolate. Conducta preferred the dark sort, with rose-scented cream inside, dribbling as she sucked out the soft pink centers. Globula had a passion for chocolate with nuts, which she gleefully crunched into pulp with her yellowing tombstone teeth. Not that they had had much access to such delights; it was many months since their father had helped himself to a large heart-shaped box of mixed centers left in a royal coach. The coach had been standing outside the blacksmith's shop while the driver negotiated terms for a new wheel; Weasel Canker had seized his opportunity and departed with a fur rug, three satin cushions, and the chocolates. Biting hard on a chocolate Brazil nut with a rotten tooth had resulted in a sudden decision to donate the box to his daughters; the rug and the cushions had been sold to a useful contact beyond the borders of the Five Kingdoms and the proceeds spent in a dark, dank, and generally unpleasant little inn on the edge of Howling Mere. Conducta and Globula, however, had tasted heaven and found the Meaning of Life.

"Out!" The rolling pin crashed against the door, and Conducta scowled. A woman passing by with a baby in her arms saw her expression and hurriedly covered the baby's eyes with her hand; the small boy trailing behind her burst into tears and clung to his mother's leg.

"Little sissy! I'll bite your nose off!" Globula hissed, and the little boy's cries ratcheted up to an ear-splitting scream of terror. His mother snatched him up and ran.

"Nasty little snot-faced brat," Conducta remarked as she tucked her arm through her sister's. "So—what are we going to do now?"

"Think of something really, really nasty to do to Ma?" Globula sounded hopeful—but Conducta shook her head.

"That can wait. No—we need money. Money—and somewhere to live. And I've got an idea."

"Tell!" Globula's tiny piggy eyes gleamed.

Her twin looked first left, then right. Satisfied that she couldn't be overheard, she whispered, "We'll go and find Great-Grandpa."

Globula opened and shut her mouth, then swallowed. "You mean . . . Dad's grandpa? The one who lives outside the border? The BAD one?"

Conducta nodded. "That's right."

"But . . . we don't even know if he's still alive!" Globula still had the expression of a startled goldfish.

"Of course he is," Conducta snapped. "Why do you think Ma never ever lets us go with Pa when he visits Grandma? It's 'cause she's scared. Scared we'll meet Great-Grandpa, and he'll turn us evil, just like he is." She gave an admiring grunt. "Fancy being so evil, you're not allowed into the Five Kingdoms!"

Globula sniggered. "Who'd want to be a goody-goody,

though? 'S much more fun pinching babies to make them scream . . ."

"And twisting arms until we get pennies," Conducta agreed.

"And throwing stones at puppies . . ."

"And sneaking plums from the market . . ."

"And spitting the stones into the village well!"

The twins grinned at each other.

Then Globula asked, "Do you know where Great-Grandpa lives? Will we be able to find the way?"

"I know which path goes to the border," Conducta told her. "After that we can ask, but it can't be far. When Pa goes to see Grandma, he's back in a day."

"Unless he gets drunk at the Howling Arms," Globula pointed out — but Conducta ignored her.

"We'll get going straightaway. If Great-Grandpa's as bad as Ma says he is, he's bound to have some ideas for making easy money. Or maybe he's got a treasure stash from when he used to turn puppy dogs into meat pies, and he'll give us a bag of gold."

"And then"— Globula stuck her grubby fingers in her mouth and sucked noisily —"we can buy CHOCOLATE!"

Conducta didn't answer. She was watching a small boy dressed as a palace page hurrying across the market square. He was clutching a piece of parchment, and even at a distance, a golden crest could easily be seen, glinting in the sunshine. It was the same crest that had adorned the large box of stolen chocolates, the box that was still the twins' most prized possession. Conducta's eyes gleamed. "I think," she said, "we might like to see what's on that piece of paper, don't you, Globula?"

Globula sniggered. "Why? Do you think it's an invitation to a ball?"

Conducta took no notice and set off toward the unsuspecting Bobby. He was trying to fix the parchment to a board with the aid of a bent nail and a rusty thumbtack and failing miserably.

"Not making much of a job of that, are you?" Conducta sneered.

Bobby jumped and looked around. "Oh! Erm . . . excuse me, miss . . ."

Globula appeared on his other side and plucked the parchment out of his hand. " 'The job of a lifetime,' " she read aloud. " 'Come and join the happy team at Niven's Knowe Palace. Two maids and a cook. Only those with the very best of references need apply. Signed, Princess Fedora. P.S. Come to the palace early tomorrow morning.' Hmph!"

"If you please, miss," Bobby said, "can I have that back? I promised I'd put it on the notice board, and if I don't get home soon, they'll be worrying."

The twins looked at each other, and an unspoken message passed between them. Then, as one, they turned back to Bobby.

"There's no need to be a worrywart." Conducta did her best to smile, and Bobby took an alarmed step backward. "Don't you fret. Just leave it to us. We'll make sure your notice gets to all the right people, won't we, Globula?"

"Oh, yes." Globula smiled, too, and cold shivers ran up and down Bobby's spine. "*All* the right people."

Bobby had a strong suspicion that the twins' idea of "the right people" was unlikely to meet with Princess Fedora's approval, but he was desperate to get away. "Well . . ." he said doubtfully. "I suppose it might be OK . . ."

"It will." Globula folded up the parchment and stuffed it deep into her pocket. "You run along."

Bobby, however, was engaged in a last-ditch battle with his conscience and didn't move. Conducta oozed nearer. "We've got a relation who works at the palace," she said in conciliatory tones. "Her name's Saturday Mousewater. She'll tell you all about us."

The cloud lifted, and Bobby felt his responsibilities drop away. "Oh, yes! She's my friend. Oh — thanks!" And he sped off toward the pie shop.

"Excellent!" A satisfied smile spread over Conducta's face. "Just wait until Ma sees that! A job at the palace . . ."

Globula was horrified. "We're not going to have to work, are we?"

Conducta gave her twin a sour look. "Don't be so stupid. Of course we aren't. We'll show Ma the parchment and tell her we've got the job. She'll stop nagging — and then we can go out all day every day and do exactly what we want."

"But . . ." Globula had spotted a problem. "What about when she asks for our wages?"

"That's why we're going to see Great-Grandpa, isn't it?" her sister snapped. "To find some way of getting money."

Globula opened and shut her mouth, a blank expression on her face. Conducta seized her by the hair and banged her head against the notice board. "Do you really think Ma's going to approve of anything Great-Grandpa suggests?"

"OW! OW!" Globula retaliated by trying to stick her fingers into her twin's eyes, and they scratched and slapped at each other until Conducta began to laugh. "What is it?" Globula asked angrily, rubbing her cheek.

"You. You're so stupid, it's funny. Come on—let's go." And Conducta marched away. After a moment Globula followed her, glowering. A large and balding crow perched on a nearby chimney pot had been observing what was going on with an expression of keen interest. As the twins set off on their journey, he gave a satisfied squawk, spread his wings, and flew off ahead of them, in the direction of the southern border.

Chapter Six

Professor Scallio was still sitting at his desk. He had spent the night in the library, and the day was now well advanced. The tottering pile of books beside him was in severe danger of falling over and crushing him, but every so often he jumped up and took yet another ancient tome from the shelves. "There must be something here," he muttered to himself. "Something that'll tell me more about dragons. What can they be looking for? What are they after?"

"Got another problem, Prof? Tell old Marlon. All inquiries treated confidential, and no questions asked where no questions needed."

Professor Scallio looked up. "Marlon? Thank heavens you're back. Have there been any more sightings?"

"Nope. Would have told you, wouldn't I?" The bat flew down and landed on the pile of books. There was a worrisome wobble before it stabilized. "Phew!" Marlon waved a wing. "Living dangerously, eh, Prof?"

"Oh—I do hope not," the professor said with a sincerity that made the bat's ears twitch. "Marlon, I've been wondering about the dragons that were driven out of Niven's Knowe. Could there be a connection, do you think? Could they be planning . . . revenge?"

"Dragons of Niven's Knowe . . ." Marlon folded his wings while he considered. "Nah. Before my time. You'd need to ask Great-Uncle Alvin. Used to live in Niven's Knowe Palace, and he's as old as the hills."

Professor Scallio leaned forward, an eager expression on his face. "Where would I find him?"

Marlon rolled his eyes. "Uncle A. had a row with my dad and fled. Ancient history. Not been seen in the Five Kingdoms for years. He's been hangin' out in a cave near Fracture, mumbling and complaining. Says the world's going to rack and ruin. Pops out from time to time to see the kid, though . . . took a shine to her, he did." Marlon gave an affectionate sigh. "That's Truehearts for you. Even ol' misery-guts raises a smile when our Gracie Gillypot's around."

The professor stroked his chin. "Ancient history . . . that's what King Horace said. Your great-uncle Alvin might know something useful."

"Doubt it," Marlon scoffed.

"Didn't he ever tell you stories about dragons when you were a baby?" The professor sounded hopeful — but the bat shook his head.

"Nope. Not a word. Deprived childhood 'n' all that."

"Poor old Dad. No one to tell you stories . . ." A smaller bat came fluttering down to join Marlon, and the pile of books gave up and collapsed to the floor with a crash. "Oops! Sorry, Professor."

Professor Scallio ignored the landslide. "Have *you* seen the dragons again, Millie?"

Millie nodded. "Saw the gold one. All on her own she was, circling in the South. You know what, Prof? I was watching her, and I think she's lost a little one. She looks just like Mum does when Freddie goes missing."

The professor stared at Millie for so long, she began to blush. "Don't look at me like that, Prof! What have I said? Didn't mean no harm. It was just a suggestion."

"Millie," the professor said slowly, "you're a genius. Why ever didn't I think of that? Of course that's what she's after." He shook his head. "I'm getting old. No doubt about it."

Millie puffed out her extremely small chest. "Just call it woman's intuition, Professor. Sometimes you men just can't see what's obvious to us girls."

Marlon coughed. "Hate to break in here, guys, but we ain't seen no baby dragons. Not a snip. Not a whisker. And we've got full surveillance out in the South."

"What? What do you mean, whiskers? *Oh!*" Professor Scallio's brow cleared. "No, no, Marlon. I didn't mean there was a baby dragon. I meant an egg. An egg laid while the dragons were still in Niven's Knowe . . . an egg that must still be out there somewhere."

"That was eighty years ago," Marlon said soothingly. "Be addled by now. No need to worry—"

"NO!" The professor jumped up from his desk. "No, *no*, NO! Eighty years is more or less how long it takes a dragon's egg to hatch." He began to pace up and down, while the two bats watched him. "An egg . . . a dragon's egg. Goodness gracious me . . . and there I was thinking they were planning some kind of revenge against King Horace."

"So that's an improvement, then," Millie said cheerfully—but Professor Scallio shook his head.

"No, no . . . this puts a whole new slant on things. Oh, dear me! A dragon's egg could be more dangerous than open warfare. If the forces of evil inside and outside the kingdoms hear about it—why, they'd do anything to get ahold of it. Sorcerers, zombies, Deep Witches, Old Trolls . . . just imagine what power they would have if they had a dragon by their side! Oh, my goodness — the whole Five Kingdoms could be destroyed!"

Marlon was looking puzzled. "Thought dragons didn't hold with evil 'n' such."

Millie nodded agreement. "Me, too."

Professor Scallio sank back into his chair. "You're quite right — they don't. Not as a rule. But a young dragon is like any other young animal. If treated with cruelty, then it will be cruel . . . and a cruel and cold-hearted dragon is more to be feared than any other beast."

There was silence while Marlon digested this information. "Well, I'll be," he said at last.

Millie, seeing the professor's evident distress, flew down to his shoulder. "It'll be OK, Professor," she told him. "You've got us on your side. And Mr. Prince and Miss Gracie. And the Ancient Crones . . ."

"Yes. Yes, let's keep hopeful. And, as far as we know, this is still our secret." The professor jumped up again and began to search through the heap of books. "And the egg may not be due to hatch for quite a while, so we have time to find it. Let me see . . . where is it . . . YES!" He began to pace again, the book in his hand. "Listen to this. 'The age of the maternal dragon must always be taken into account in any estimation of hatching time. A dragoness of sixty years should not expect to see her offspring until some seventy years have passed. A dragoness aged eighty must wait ninety years' . . . and so on. You see? If we could find out how old the golden dragon is, we'd know when her egg is due to hatch."

"If there *is* an egg," Marlon put in.

"Yes, of course." The professor nodded. "But I think we should assume there is, for the time being at least. Marlon, you must find your great-uncle Alvin and ask him to tell us everything he knows."

"Ah." The bat shuffled up and down the arm of the professor's chair. "Might be a problem. Ol' misery-guts ain't speaking to me just now. Bit of an argument, see."

Millie gave her father a reproachful look, and Professor Scallio visibly drooped. "Oh, dear . . ."

There was another silence, and then Marlon coughed. "Ahem. Gotta suggestion. Like I said, the aged unc would do anything for Gracie. Tell her all he knows and most likely a whole lot more as well." The bat gave the professor a sideways glance. "And you could trust her. Trueheart through and through, that one."

"You're right!" The professor sat up straighter. "Marcus was off to see her today. Maybe I should ask the two of them to go together. . . ."

"Good plan, Stan!" Marlon's eyes brightened. "Nobody'll take a second glance at those two wandering around. They're just kids. Uncle A will deliver the goods, and that'll be that. You know what, Prof? I'll lay an even fiver that this time next week you won't have a worry in the world."

Marlon's optimism was catching, and Professor Scallio smiled as he took off his monocle and polished it. "You're on! I'll take your bet, and we'll hope you're right. Could you tell Marcus and Gracie that I'd like to see them here? No. No, on second thought, just tell them what we have in mind. Much better that way. Saves unnecessary travel. And, Marlon—speak to the Ancient Crones. Ask them if they've seen any sign of trouble on the web."

"No prob." Marlon flew a swift circle around the library. "Coming, kid?"

Millie shook her head. "I'd better get back to the border, Dad. Got to keep an eye out for that poor dragon."

Her father waved a wing. "Old softie, ain't she! Be back pronto, Prof." And Marlon was gone. Moments later, Millie set off for the border.

The professor watched them go. "I hope I'm not putting Marcus and Gracie in danger . . . but I really

don't think there's any chance of that. Heigh-ho . . .
how tired I am!" And he laid his head on the book in
front of him and fell fast asleep. Even the crash of the
door as Queen Bluebell came marching in failed to
wake him.

The queen looked down in surprise at the tumbled
heaps of books and the sleeping professor. "Whatever's
going on?" she asked the empty library. "Never seen
such a mess. Aha! So that's where I left it!" She retrieved
her lorgnette with a grunt of satisfaction. Curiosity
made her peer at the book under the professor's nose.
"Hmph! It's those dragons again. Well, I never. Think
the poor old chap needs a vacation. I'll send him off
to that sister of his. Do him good to have a rest." And
with a decisive shake of her head, she left the professor
to sleep.

Chapter Seven

Conducta and Globula had found their way to the southern border of the Five Kingdoms relatively easily. They had persuaded a farmer driving an empty cart to give them a lift for much of the way; the farmer had not intended to go nearly so far — or, indeed, so fast — but his old gray horse had spooked when Globula began to whistle, and it had taken the farmer six or seven miles to persuade the animal to calm down to a manageable speed.

"That's some whistle you've got there," he said sourly as the girls climbed down.

"Isn't it?" Globula agreed. As the farmer turned the cart, Globula winked at Conducta, put her fingers in her mouth, and blew a high-pitched whistle that only the horse could hear. The cart disappeared in a cloud of dust, and the twins collapsed into giggles.

"Wish I could whistle like that," Conducta said as they climbed the wooden stile that marked the border crossing. A couple of ancient guards yawned, gave the twins a cursory glance, and then went on with their knitting.

"You can spit farther than I can," Globula reminded her sister as they walked on.

"I can, can't I?" Conducta gave a demonstration— then stopped as a movement caught her eye. "What's that bird doing?"

A large and balding crow had flapped down from a twisted elm that sheltered the path. He tilted his head to one side and studied first Conducta and then Globula with an evil little eye. "You'll be Cankers, then. Yer great-grandpa said you'd be along one day. Taken yer time. You'd best follow me."

For once the twins were at a loss for words.

The crow gave a harsh screech by way of a laugh and hopped closer. "Never met a bird like me before, I'll bet."

"Erm . . . no." Conducta pulled herself together and into her normal state of narrow-eyed wariness. "How do we know you're going to take us the right way? And what makes you think we're Cankers? We might be Mousewaters for all you know!"

The crow gave a louder screech of laughter. "Mousewaters! Since when did a Mousewater spit like that? And what Mousewater ever drove a horse mad, thinking it had a wasp in its ear, just by whistling? Nah. Cankers through and through, you two are. Yer great-grandpa'll be pleased as Punch. Feared you were growing up soft and sappy like that Mousewater mother of yours. Never once been to see him, have you?"

"Ma wouldn't let us." Globula folded her arms. "And Great-Grandpa never came to see us, either."

This made the crow laugh so much, he had to lean against the trunk of the tree to recover. At last he said, "You're a scream, you are. Don't they teach you nothing in those schools of yours? Don't they teach you that that border"—he waved a ragged wing in the direction of the stile—"is as far as your grandpappy can go? If he as much as thought of showing up in yer goody-goody world, those hideous old crones would be onto him, and the armies would be sent out, and he'd be marched off and away forever. Now, are you going to follow me or stand here yakking all day?"

"We'll follow you." The twins spoke together, and the crow began to half fly, half hop between the trees. Globula poked Conducta in the ribs as they hurried behind him. "What's Grandma like?"

The crow heard her and swiveled his head to answer. "You don't need to worry about that old bag. Nothing left of her but skin and bones and a vinegar tongue."

Conducta made a face. "So why does Dad bother to come and see her?"

"Where's yer wits?" There was another screech. "He comes to see if the old man's OK, of course. Could be your dad'll be thrown out as well, one of these days. Seen him up to a few naughty little tricks, I have . . . and he's not as careful as he should be. Singing rude songs outside the Howling Arms is only the start of it." The crow found this hilariously funny, and Conducta and Globula had to wait while he laughed himself in and out of a coughing fit. When he could speak again, he asked, "Brought yer granpappy a present, have you? He likes presents. Makes him happy."

"No." Globula frowned. "Why should we bring him presents? He's never given us anything."

The crow gave her a knowing wink. "Might be to yer advantage to keep him happy, Miss Clever Clogs. Seeing as you're wanting to ask him a favor, like."

"How do you know that?" Conducta glared at him.

"I hear things." The crow nodded his bald head. "And I see things. They can't keep us birds out of the Five Kingdoms, you know."

Globula began to dig in her pockets. At last she pulled out a small and somewhat battered brooch. "Would this do?"

Conducta grinned. "That belongs to Ma! It's her favorite!"

"I know." Her sister was looking smug. "Given to Ma by her poor old ancient mother as she lay breathing her last Mousewatery breath. I took it yesterday when she was nagging on and on and on. Serves her right for being so mean."

"That'll do nicely." The crow sounded impressed. "Right . . . here we are. After you, ladies. I suggest you keep to the path. Fall off it, and you'll be sucked down into the Ravenous Bog, and I doubt you'll ever be seen again." And he swept a mocking bow to them, then pointed with his ragged wing at a small and winding path that made its way between pools of stagnant green water and blackened roots.

Globula hesitated, but Conducta pushed past her and grabbed her hand. "Come on," she said. "We've come this far. We may as well see what the old man's like."

Above their heads, the crow, now perched on a rotten and ivy-strangled tree, gave a series of loud squawks that could have been meant either as encouragement or derision.

Conducta ignored him. "I can see a house!"

To call the broken-down hovel that was set in the midst of the scum-encrusted water a "house" was beyond complimentary. The roof was thatched with a patchwork of sodden rushes, tattered pieces of old cloth, bent and rusty wire, and what appeared to be long skeins of dirty brown, black, and reddish yarn. It was only as the twins came closer that they saw this was, in fact, hair. Human hair woven in and out to hold the rickety roof together. The twins paused, and at that moment a tiny shrunken creature appeared in the darkness of the doorway. As soon as she saw them, she put a bony finger to her lips, then waved her arms as if shooing them away.

Conducta stood her ground. "Are you Grandma? Dad's mother?"

The creature nodded.

"Well—we've come to see our great-grandpa. Please tell him we're here."

"His Malignancy is taking a rest. His Malignancy is sleeping now." The creature's voice was monotonous and curiously metallic; Conducta found herself rubbing at her ears.

Globula was made of sterner stuff. She put her fingers in her mouth and whistled.

The skeletal figure gave a faint cry and disappeared. From the darkness inside the hovel, another voice, a voice that appeared to have its own hollow echo, boomed, "My little darlings! Come and kiss your old granpappy. Come inside, my lovely little cankerous ones . . ."

Conducta looked at Globula, and Globula looked at Conducta. Then they linked arms and went in through the door. A small candle was flickering in the gloom, but at first they could see nothing—nothing but a huge mass of old rags heaped on the damp earth floor.

"Come a little closer," said the voice. "Granpappy is waiting. Waiting for his kisses. . . ."

Chapter Eight

Marcus had left Gorebreath Palace early, despite a gloomy sky. Buoyed up by his mission, he had set off at breakneck speed; only concern for his pony made him slow down as he made his way through the Enchanted and Less Enchanted Forests.

It was a route he and the pony knew well, and as the Five Kingdoms fell far behind, the prince began to whistle. His home life, with all its rules and regulations and restrictions, bored him unutterably; he was profoundly grateful that his twin, Prince Arioso, would inherit the crown and the kingdom. *Although I would be able to bring in a few dragons if I were king,* he thought idly. *But maybe I could persuade Arry.* Further consideration made him regretfully decide that this was beyond unlikely, and he began dreaming of a life of exploration instead.

"*Cooee!* Marcus!"

Marcus jumped, and Glee broke into an eager canter. Gracie was waving from the top of the path, Gubble standing foursquare beside her.

"Hi, Gubble!" Marcus said as he slid off Glee's back. "Hello, Gracie. How did you know I was coming?"

Gracie grinned. "Alf," she said. "He raced you here."

A cheery squeaking from a neighboring tree confirmed that Alf was not only present but extremely pleased with himself. "Remembered you were off on a jaunt today, Mr. Prince! Thought you'd got me beat, but you slowed down on those hills."

"I've got a picnic." Gracie pointed to the large wicker basket on the grass beside her. "Although the weather doesn't look too good." She glanced up at the cloudy sky. "Still—we might be lucky. Oh, Auntie Edna says to be sure and bring you back for tea." She paused for a moment, then went on: "Alf says you were in Wadingburn Palace library yesterday, and you were talking about dragons."

Marcus grimaced. "You know what? I'd really hate to try to keep a secret from you and the Ancient Crones. What with Marlon and Millie and Alf whizzing to and fro, you know everything just about as soon as it happens!"

Gracie, always sensitive to other people's feelings, realized he had wanted to tell her the news himself. "Alf didn't say much, really. He says he went back to sleep when Queen Bluebell and King Horace appeared." She gave Alf a warning glance, and the little bat took the hint and settled himself to listen.

"Well . . ." Marcus draped one arm casually over Glee's saddle and the other over Gracie's shoulders. "Arry and Nina-Rose were driving me mad, so I went to see the prof . . ."

"Ug." Gubble, realizing this was likely to be a long story, picked up the picnic basket. "Gubble carry. Go to pool." Without waiting for the others to agree, he turned and made his way up a small side path.

Glee followed him, and Gracie and Marcus, still talking, went where the pony led them. By the time Gubble had reached his favorite picnic spot, Gracie had heard all about the dragons and the professor's concerns, as well as Marcus's idea for her birthday.

"Do you think the dragons are planning to attack the Five Kingdoms?" Marcus asked. "I wouldn't blame them, actually. I can't believe they were chucked out. But why haven't they done it before? I wouldn't think anything as powerful as a dragon would be bothered by those stupid laws."

Gracie sucked the end of her braid. "I don't know. It sounds more as if they're looking for something. Or someone. We'll ask the aunts when we get back."

"Oh! I've just remembered!" Marcus slapped his hand on Glee's saddle. "The prof said I was to ask his sister about the web of power."

"Auntie Val?" Gracie looked surprised. "Oh — of course. Hmm . . . do you think he's told her more about the dragons than he's told you?"

"He might have," Marcus said. "You could ask her."

Gracie was thinking out loud: "The professor's right. The web *has* been a bit odd lately. Auntie Edna's not said much, but I can tell she's worried. She might be quite relieved to hear about the dragons, actually — I think she's scared there's some kind of horrible evil brewing." She sat down underneath the tree where Gubble, now completely surrounded by crumbs, had settled himself.

Marcus, with a suppressed sigh, sat down beside her. Picnics were overly domestic in his view; he preferred action and adventure.

Gracie pulled the picnic basket toward her. "Would you like a sandwich — oh! They're nearly all gone! There's not a single egg one left, and they're my favorite. Gubble? Have you eaten all the egg sandwiches?"

Gubble looked up, his cheeks bulging. "Ug." He sounded reproachful. "Gubble hungry."

"Hmm." Gracie was inspecting the remains. "Sorry, Marcus. The chocolate cake's gone, too. There's a fruitcake left—hang on a minute. It's got a huge bite out of it! Gubble . . . how *could* you?"

The troll stared down at his toes. "Bad Gubble. Gracie angry. Gracie hate Gubble."

"Heavens, no." Gracie patted his arm reassuringly.

A puzzled expression crossed Gubble's flat green face. "Niven's Knowe?"

Gracie realized his mistake. "No . . . I said, 'Heavens, no.' I meant I wasn't angry. Just a bit disappointed. I'm ever so hungry, and Auntie Elsie makes the best egg sandwiches ever."

"More egg at home," Gubble suggested. "Go home."

"That's an idea," Marcus said eagerly. "We can tell your aunts about the dragons and ask about the web."

"I've always wanted to see a dragon." Gracie shook the last crumbs out of the picnic basket. Without looking at Marcus, she added, "That was a nice idea of yours to take me to see a—What was it? A flight?—a flight of dragons for my birthday."

Marcus shuffled his feet. "Oh. Good. I mean, I just wanted to do something special." There was a pause, and then he said rather quickly, "You see, you're a bit special, Gracie."

"Wheeeeeeeee!" As Gracie blushed, Alf looped an enthusiastic loop over her head. "Go on, Mr. Prince! Go on! Give her a kiss!"

Marcus turned an agonized scarlet, and Gracie all but shut herself in the picnic basket.

Alf looped another loop. "Wheeeeeeee!" he caroled, "Wheee— OOF!"

There was a small but solid *thump* as Gubble put up his hand and checked Alf midflight. "'Nuff," he said firmly. "Bad bat."

Alf, lying on his back on the grass, glared up at him. He was too winded to speak. Marcus began to laugh loudly, and Gracie looked at him in surprise. Realizing he was only trying to cover his embarrassment, she joined in. Gubble stared at them before trying out a few puzzled chuckles himself.

"It would serve Alf right if we shut him in the basket," Gracie said with feeling, and she gave Marcus a rueful smile.

Marcus breathed again. *Good old Gracie,* he thought. *All the other girls I know would have made a terrible fuss. But she's different.*

Alf managed a hoarse squeak.

"He's sorry," Gracie interpreted. "Come on. Let's go back to the house. It looks as if it's about to rain."

She was right. As the small party emerged from the trees, a few drops began to fall, followed by more and more. By the time they reached the House of the Ancient Crones, they were soaked through.

"We can't go in through the front door, I'm afraid," Gracie said as she negotiated the path, which was twirling around her ankles in a loving but irritating way. "It's been behaving very badly recently. It's spent the last two days up on the roof. Maybe we should go around to the back, and then you can put Glee in the stable before we go inside."

They dripped their way around the outside of the house, and after drying Glee with a wisp of straw and settling him comfortably, they headed for the back door. The front door had slid down beside it and was flapping its mailbox in an inviting manner. Gracie looked at it suspiciously. "Last time it did that, it tried to pinch my fingers. I think we'll use the other one."

Marcus, who was used to doors staying where they were, was happy to agree. He, Gracie, and Gubble trailed inside and immediately found themselves in the kitchen. There was a roaring fire in the hearth and a kettle singing on the stove; Marcus's and Gracie's spirits rose, and Gubble grunted approval.

The Youngest One was stirring a large saucepan of delicious-smelling soup, and she nodded knowingly. "Thought the rain would send you home, so I've made some soup. Or did you have time to eat your picnic?"

"Gubble did," Gracie said as she handed Marcus a towel. "He ate all the sandwiches and the chocolate cake. I think he only left the fruitcake because he doesn't like raisins. Marcus and I are starving. That smells wonderful!"

Val smiled. "Good. Do you want some bread?"

"Yes, please," Gracie said — and then feeling Marcus's eyes on her, she added, "Did you know Professor Scallio's been watching out for dragons, Auntie Val?"

Val looked at her in surprise. "Dragons? Frederick? No. I had no idea."

It was Gracie's turn to look surprised. "Oh . . . I thought he might have told you."

"He's been overworking, if you ask me." Val gave the soup a final stir. "He's got some research he's working on, or so he says. Sent Millie with a message that he wouldn't be home last night. Him and his books!" The youngest crone shook her head in sisterly despair.

"Now, when you've had something to eat, the Ancient One wants to have a word with you. Marlon's just arrived, and the two of them are hatching some wild idea." Val looked disapproving. "Seems he wants you two to go off on some expedition or other. And instead of telling him not to talk nonsense, Edna's all for it." She stopped to pour soup into two large bowls.

"An expedition? Where?" Marcus jumped up from the table — but Val waved him down again.

"Now then, Mr. Prince — you sit down and eat your soup. You can't go anywhere on an empty stomach, and, besides, Edna and Marlon are still talking. Plenty of time to find out all about it once you've eaten."

Gracie grinned at Marcus. "You'd better do as Auntie Val says. She worked as a nanny before she came to the House of the Ancient Crones." She did not think it necessary to explain that the Youngest had, in those distant days, also been in the habit of regularly absconding with all the children's toys. Val's ways had been radically changed by the Ancient One, and she was now a reformed character, as was Elsie. Gracie's stepsister, Foyce, was currently undergoing the same process; her progress was slow, but the Ancient One was not without hope.

Marcus sighed but did as he was told.

Chapter Nine

Globula and Conducta were not enjoying their visit to their great-grandfather. After kissing his cold slimy face, they had each been kissed in return; both twins had furtively wiped the chilly slobber from their cheeks as they stepped back.

"Sit down now, my little darlings, and we will talk," their granpappy told them. He lifted a formless fleshy arm, and their legs gave way under them. As there were no chairs, they were obliged to sink down among the heaps of sodden rubbish, moldering rags, bits of rotting paper, and some indefinable sticky substance that seemed to be spreading out from Old Malignancy himself. From time to time, there were furtive slitherings that were far too close for the twins' comfort; they were more than happy to put a handful of slugs (carefully chosen for excessive size and sliminess) in the pockets of a teacher or an unsuspecting child, but to see silvery trails circling their feet was an entirely different proposition. There was also a remarkable number of worms. Both Conducta and Globula had forced many of their little friends at school to eat worms, but those were of the common pink variety. These were longer and squirmier and a curious greenish white. They gleamed in the faint light from the doorway, and the twins found themselves pulling their dresses closer around their bony thighs.

"Ho, ho, ho!" Granpappy Canker was laughing, but his laughter had no warmth in it. "My little cankerettes don't like the company I keep, I see. Well, I never. And there I was thinking you'd done away with those nasty finicky Mousewater ways! Too good for me, are you, my persnickety darlings? Had to wipe away your dear old granpappy's kisses?"

Conducta shifted guiltily but didn't answer. Globula felt it was the right time to pull out her mother's brooch. "Here, Granpappy," she said. "We brought you this."

"Ahhhhh . . ." Old Malignancy sighed, and it was a sigh of pleasure. "Perhaps I was wrong. Your mother's brooch, I see. Now, that pleases me, my dears. That pleases me very much. She will be crying and wailing and missing that little gift, and those cries and wails will

be music to my ears." He stretched out his flabby white hand, and, as Globula gave him the brooch, Conducta rubbed her eyes. Was it her imagination, or had her great-grandfather grown larger? Before she could make up her mind, he crushed the little trinket between his fingers and a cloud of bright dust floated into the air before vanishing into the darkness. When he opened his hand again, the brooch was gone. There was, however, a bright red welt on Old Malignancy's palm. He had also, Conducta noticed, shrunk back to his former size.

"Well, I never . . . what a lot of goodness there was in that brooch. And love." Old Malignancy's voice was as sharp as lemon juice in a cut. "We must remember to beware of Mousewaters. A hint of Trueheart in their ancestry, it would seem . . . dear me. How very unpleasant." He gave the twins such a cold look that they shrank back. "Let us hope, my precious cankerettes, that such an affliction has passed you by."

"We're just like our dad," Conducta told him. She was annoyed to hear that her voice had a tremor in it and tried again. "Mum's always telling us."

Globula's attention had been caught by something else. "What's a Trueheart?"

Old Malignancy shuddered. It was difficult to see where he began and ended, but the shuddering filled the room until even the walls shook and the twins' teeth rattled in their heads. Conducta clutched her sister's hand, and Globula shut her eyes. "We will not speak the word again," Old Malignancy said as the shuddering subsided to a faint tremble. "They stand in the way of Evil, my little dears. . . . They stand in the way of Evil, and each one must be shredded into many thousands of pieces before the glorious way of Evil lies clear before us. But you are here for a reason, and you meant well by bringing me a gift. What do you want of me?"

The twins looked at each other. This was more like it. This was why they had come. "Granpappy," Conducta began, "we need money." She pulled the parchment out of her pocket. "Ma wants us to get jobs, but we're Cankers." She gave a sly smile. "We don't work, not like stupid people. But we need a way of getting money."

Globula nodded. "We've got a plan. We're going to tell Ma we're working at the palace, but—"

"Let me see." Old Malignancy took the parchment from Conducta and studied it before handing it back. Something like a smile crept over his bloated face, and he gave a mirthless chuckle. "How very interesting. A position at the palace."

"Of course, we're not *really* going to work there," Conducta explained. "We're much too clever for that—"

"Oh, no, my little canker. Not so very clever." There was something in his voice that made the twins shiver. "If you were clever, you would not have come to find me. By coming here, you have made yourselves mine, and now you must do as I tell you."

Conducta and Globula opened their mouths to say they had no intention of doing anything they didn't want to, but the words froze on their lips. "Errrr . . ." they said. "Errrr . . ."

Their great-grandfather chuckled coldly. "You see? Now, listen. You will go to the palace, and you will ask for work. And you will lurk and linger and spy, and you will tell me why there are no servants at Niven's Knowe. It seems to me that there must be unhappiness there, and dissent, and that interests me. . . . It interests me very much. Perhaps you might care to spread a little more. Anger and resentment can be as catching as the measles if the flames are stirred. So much fun, my little cankerettes. SO much fun!"

This was far more to the twins' liking. They nodded enthusiastically, and Old Malignancy smiled his chilly smile.

"So now we understand each other. I will consider this further . . . consider it carefully. But now I am tired. Run along, my dears, and come back and see me soon. Very soon, and then we will talk more."

The twins, released from whatever strange force had been holding them, got to their feet. They began to make their way toward the door — but greed made Conducta brave. "And you'll give us lots of money if we do as you say, Granpappy?"

Their great-grandfather gave her a look that was half despising, half admiring. "You have your father's spirit, my dear. There may well be rewards for you . . . if you do as you are told."

"Oh, we *will*!" Conducta promised with her fingers crossed behind her back, and she gave a cheerful wave as she and Globula walked out into the daylight.

Behind her, Old Malignancy gave another chuckle as he sank into his bed. He lifted a hand, and Carrion came sidling in, his wicked little eyes gleaming. "Met their dear ol' granpappy, then. Sly young ladies, them two. Take after you, I'd say."

"Follow them to Niven's Knowe," Old Malignancy ordered. "Watch them, and watch the palace, too. No . . . wait." He paused, and the crow, who knew him well, gave an encouraging squawk. "Tell me, Carrion: 'two housemaids and a cook.' Am I right?"

"That's what the paper said," the crow agreed.

"Then there is, as one might say, an unusual opportunity." Old Malignancy sounded thoughtful. "An opportunity that may never come again." His eyes, sunk deep in rolls of pale flesh, glittered. "Oh, that I could make my way into the palace. To be inside . . . oh, how I would corrupt and poison and bind them to me. . . ."

Carrion gave a harsh laugh. "Ain't you forgetting? You're banned! Laws of the Five Kingdoms."

"I never forget." The glittering eyes turned on the crow. "Never. But kings and queens make the laws, and kings and queens can change their minds."

"True." Carrion tweaked a tail feather into place. "Amazin' how a mind can change. 'Specially when a bit of discomfort's involved. Couple of broken toes. Bump on the head. A few missing teeth. Never fails to surprise me how the human mind can turn right around when the owner's likely to lose a tooth or two."

Old Malignancy tapped the crow on his beak with a surprisingly long, thin finger. "But there are other ways, Carrion. Far more subtle ways. To creep into their bodies . . . to seep into their minds . . . that is true corruption."

"If you say so." Carrion nodded. "Go on, then. What was you thinking of?"

There was a deep hollow laugh. "Sending my sister to the palace of Niven's Knowe."

The crow looked up in surprise. "Sister? What sister? I ain't never heard you mention no sister."

"There are sisters, and there are sisters. Her name is . . . what shall we say?" There was a thoughtful pause. "'Mercy Grinder.' Yes. That will do very well."

Carrion put his head on one side. "And what's this Mercy Grinder going to do exactly?"

Old Malignancy leaned forward. "She will cook . . . and, oh, what a cook she will make!" His shapeless body quivered and shook with silent laughter. "What a cook! Early tomorrow morning, she will cross the border, Carrion. Mercy Grinder is not banned from the Five Kingdoms, you see. Mercy Grinder is a cook, on her way to the palace of Niven's Knowe."

The crow shifted from foot to foot. "What about them guards? Not a lot of use, I know, but they'll still ask questions. Can't cross the border without an invite, you know."

One pale eye winked. "Correct me if I am wrong, dear Carrion, but did the advertisement not conclude with the words 'Come to the palace early tomorrow morning'? Written in the princess's very own handwriting, no less? And then there was a seal. A very fine seal. The sort of seal that makes foolish guards believe that Royalty Has Spoken. I can tell you, Carrion, that the guards will believe in Mercy Grinder. What is more, she will inform them that she will speak well of them if she is treated with courtesy, so naturally they will escort her across the border . . . and thus the power of the web will be rendered impotent!"

Carrion gave an admiring squawk. "You're a one, you are! I get it!"

The eye winked a second time. "Carrion, you are my second self. Fly now, and take that parchment from my little cankerettes."

"Good as done," Carrion cawed. "Good as done!"

As the twins' great-grandfather sank back into the darkness, the crow spread his tattered wings, flew up into the air, and circled away from the house. From a vantage point in a tall beech tree, he could see the twins hurrying along the path. It had begun to rain, but as yet they were protected by the cover of the trees. Their voices reached him easily; he clicked his beak as he listened.

"Phew!" Conducta said. "What a horror! He looked like a hideous old balloon."

Globula gave a nervous giggle. "It was a bit scary. I didn't expect him to be quite so . . . so weird."

Conducta spat neatly into a bush, and an outraged rabbit leaped out and dashed away into the distance, the top of his head stinging as if it had been burned. "I don't care. Just as long as we get some money. Lots and lots and lots of money."

"So are we going to go to the palace and ask for jobs?" Globula wanted to know. "It sounds awfully like hard work."

Conducta thought about it. "I s'pose we could. I like the idea of being a spy."

"And making people angry is *fun*," Globula pointed out.

Her sister pulled out the parchment and inspected it. "It says to come to the palace early tomorrow morning. Oof!" She looked up into the sky. "Bother. It's raining. We're going to get soaked going home."

Globula made a face. "Does 'first thing' mean we have to get up early?"

"Of course it does. Don't be stupid." Conducta gave her sister a sharp slap. Globula slapped her back, and Fedora's advertisement fell to the ground. As Conducta turned to pick it up, she was distracted by a rumbling sound. A heavily laden hay wagon was trundling along the rutted track, heading in the direction of the border. A brightly painted sign on the wagon's side proclaimed that it belonged to Jason Honeyseed, Golden Green Farm, Niven's Knowe.

"Come on," Globula urged, the fight forgotten. "We can get a lift home!" As the wagon passed them, they swung themselves onto the back and, after a certain amount of wriggling, made themselves comfortable under the tarpaulin.

Conducta grinned at her twin. "This is much better than walking. We'll be home well before dark."

"Ma'll be pleased when we tell her we're going to the palace," Globula said drowsily.

Conducta raised her eyebrows. "Since when have you cared what Ma thought?"

Her twin yawned. "I was thinking she'd cook us an extra-special tea. And if she's pleased, we can ask for everything we want. I'm hungry."

"Oh. Yes, me too," Conducta agreed, and then she also began to drift away into a land of rose-scented chocolate creams.

Carrion watched the wagon as it trundled steadily away, a calculating expression in his sharp black eyes. "Chips off the old block, all right," he mused. "Nasty little bits of work. Just what we like!" And he picked up the parchment and flew back to report his success.

Chapter Ten

Fedora's lunch had been completely inedible. Tertius had done his best, partly because he loved her and partly because he knew only too well that he would have to pay for any lack of enthusiasm once he and his bride were alone together. King Horace made no pretense at all. "Good thing I had that steak-and-kidney pie," he announced as he pushed away his plate of raw onion, congealed half-cooked eggs, and burned pastry. "Tell you what, Feddy, m'dear: you could do a lot worse than pop around to dear old Mrs. Basket and ask her for a few tips." This suggestion was met with such a remarkable drop in temperature that even the king noticed. "Hmm. Well. Must go and see to a spot of royal business." And he stomped off to his private study, where he settled himself in his favorite chair, put his feet on the mantelpiece, and went to sleep.

Tertius, left alone in an atmosphere that even a polar bear would have found depressingly chilly, tried to hide his pastry under his knife. Fedora watched him, ready to pounce, but held back from actual comment as she was unable to finish her own meal. When he began trying to balance the onion on top of his knife, she gave a loud martyred sigh. "Do you know how long I spent making you this delicious lunch, Terty?"

Given that it was nearly four o'clock and Fedora had begun her activities in the kitchen at midday, Tertius had a fair idea, but he thought it best not to say so. "Dearest one," he said, "it's very very kind of you to have taken so much trouble, and please don't think I don't appreciate it . . . but I don't think I'm terribly hungry just now."

Fedora hesitated and then gave in. "That's all right, Terty darling. I'm not very hungry, either." A brilliant idea flashed into her mind. "Tell you what—why don't we go and visit Mother? We'd be just in time for high tea." Realizing that this contradicted her earlier remark, she hastily added, "The fresh air will give us an appetite."

Tertius leaped up from the table with enthusiasm. "You're such a clever little poppet! Yes—that's a

wonderful idea. I'll just tell Father, and then we can go."
With a light step and a rumbling stomach, he hurried
down the corridor to his father's study. "Father! Feddy
and I are going to Dreghorn! We'll be back later."

"Hmph? Dragon? What? Did you say dragon?"
King Horace, woken much too suddenly, sat up with
his crown askew and his hair on end. "Dearie me. Was
having a dreadful dream. All about dragons. Terrible.
Simply terrible. Dragons running wild all over the
place. All that young Prince Marcus's fault. Dreamed
one popped out of Mrs. Basket's chicken pie. Shockin'.
And another one—" Tertius made a sympathetic sort
of noise by way of interruption, and his father came
back to the present moment. "Did you say you were
going out?"

His son nodded. "We're going to Dreghorn. You'll
be all right, won't you?"

King Horace looked plaintive. "But what'll I have
for my tea?"

"Bobby'll make you toast," Tertius told him. "And
you can always go see Mrs. Basket. Take your umbrella,
though; it's raining again."

"Mrs. Basket? Good idea." The king relaxed. "Did
I tell you I found Trout and the other servants there?
Well, not that girl—what's her name? Saturday? She's

still here. But all the others were there." A happy smile floated across his face. "Rather fun, don't you know. Might wander over and have a game of checkers with Trout later on."

"Good idea," Tertius said. "See you later, Father!" And he hurried off, to find his beloved tapping her foot as she waited in the royal traveling carriage. "Here I am, dearest Feddy!"

"You were ages," Fedora said crossly as the coach began to roll down the drive. "I've told the coachman to go as fast as he can."

"No, I wasn't," Tertius argued. "I just waited a moment while Father told me about a horrible dream he'd had, that's all."

Fedora sniffed. "I expect he had indigestion after Mrs. Basket's pie."

"Actually," Tertius said, "it was a beastly nightmare about dragons."

"Dragons?" Fedora sniffed again. "Definitely indigestion."

As the door closed, King Horace went back to sleep.

He was woken at five, by Bobby. "Toast, Your Maj?"

"Yes, please." The king stretched. "Still on your own, are you?"

Bobby grinned. "Just me and Saturday Mousewater. Been playing hide-and-seek all over the palace." A worried look crossed his face. "That's OK, isn't it, King H.?"

"Of course, of course." King Horace nodded. "Word of warning, though. Not a good idea when my daughter-in-law's about. Pretty little thing, but fussy. Got this book of rules, don't you know. All Don'ts and not many Dos, far as I can see. Still, sure it'll all turn out for the best."

There was a broad grin on Bobby's face as he began to leave the room, but as he reached the doorway, he hesitated. "Erm . . . sorry to bother you, King H., but . . . can I ask you something?"

The king looked up in surprise. "What's the matter? Broken something, have you?"

"No. But that paper—the one Princess F. asked me to put up in the marketplace. A couple of girls took it away. . . . D'you reckon that's OK? They were a bit peculiar, if you know what I mean. But they said Saturday knew them. Relations or something."

King Horace was doubtful. What would Fedora say? But then a splendid thought came to him. If there were no applicants, surely then he could persuade the pretty little thing to reinstate his own well-loved servants.

"That's fine," he said firmly. "Don't you worry about it. Now, let's have that toast."

Bobby trotted away, and the king made his plans for the rest of the evening. After eating his toast, he decided, he would wander across the park to see what Mrs. Basket was cooking. And if Trout was there, so much the better. A game of checkers after a good meal would be perfect. And perhaps he could make sure he was safely tucked up in bed before Tertius and Fedora got back.

King Horace pulled himself together with an effort. He was, he told himself firmly, very fond of his new daughter-in-law. Seeing Bobby coming back through the door with a plate piled high, he decided to concentrate on the good things in life. He did, however, resolve to leave Mrs. Basket's house in plenty of time to allow for an early night.

Bobby, after a happy half hour spent eating the king's crusts with a quite excessive amount of butter, went back to the kitchen.

Saturday Mousewater was staring into the flames of the kitchen range, and she jumped as he came in. "'Tis very lonely, only us being here, like." Her voice was quiet.

Bobby sat himself on the table, his legs swinging.

"There'll be more of us tomorrow. Princess F. sent me to put a notice up in the marketplace. Met a couple of your relations, by the way. Odd-looking girls, they were. Twins."

Saturday looked puzzled. "They said as they was related? To me?"

"Yep."

"I suppose as they might be cousins." Saturday frowned. "Twenty-eight aunties I have, so it's not impossible, like. My ol' gran did tell me a tale once of an auntie who upped and married a dreadful scary man, but she never did tell me his name. A lot of drinking, that's what he got up to. And singing songs. Songs that were"—Saturday dropped her voice to a whisper—"not nice to hear, if you gets my meaning."

"Let's hope it's nothing to do with him, then." Bobby jumped down. "Fancy another game of hide-and-seek?"

"Are you sure 'tis all right?" Saturday's eyes were wide. "Don't want to get into no trouble, like."

"Sure as sure. His Maj is out, and we'll hear soon enough when the others get back. You hide, and I'll count to a hundred!"

Chapter Eleven

It wasn't until the following morning that Gracie and Marcus set off on their expedition to find Marlon's great-uncle Alvin. All three of the Ancient Crones had advised against traveling in the pouring rain, and Marlon had volunteered to take a message to Professor Scallio explaining that Marcus was going to stay the night. The professor would then pass the message on to Gorebreath Palace, even though Marcus was convinced his devoted parents would not give his absence a second thought.

"They're much too busy looking after Nina-Rose," he explained to Edna as he and Gracie washed up the pots and pans after the evening meal. "And all Arry does is gaze at her with soupy eyes and tell her how lovely she is. He wouldn't notice if I was missing for weeks on end. Yuck. It's all pretty disgusting, if you ask me."

The Ancient One gave him a thoughtful look. "Hmm. Well, I think we'll play it safe. After what Marlon's told me, the last thing we want are royal armies tramping all over the kingdoms, looking for a missing prince. Now, remember, both of you: if Marlon's great-uncle *does* happen to know anything about the dragons, you're to go straight to Wadingburn to tell the professor. You can send Alf to tell me."

Marcus stared at her. "But what if the egg's due to hatch? I've worked it all out from what Marlon said. If the dragon was seventy when the dragons were thrown out and that was eighty years ago, then the egg should hatch any minute—"

Edna held up a hand for silence, her blue eye stern. "At this precise moment, Prince Marcus, we don't even know that there *is* an egg, so I see no point in worrying about that particular possibility. Neither do we know the age of the Niven's Knowe dragons, so any speculation is a waste of time." And soon afterward she suggested that Marcus go off to bed, in a tone of voice that allowed for no refusal.

Gracie lingered downstairs, aware that the Ancient One was far more troubled than she was admitting. "Are you all right, Auntie Edna?"

Edna gave her a fond half smile. "Bless the child.

That's the trouble with Truehearts. They always see through to the truth. No, dear, I'm worried. Worried sick—but don't tell that prince of yours. He's a good boy, but he's not as steady as you. He thinks it's all a fantastic adventure, whereas I'm afraid things might get rather serious." She sat down at the kitchen table. "I'm almost sure that there is a dragon's egg somewhere in the Five Kingdoms, and I believe the dragons are beginning to look for it; the way Marlon described their behavior would fit perfectly. And if the powers of evil find out—well. Then there'll be terrible trouble. They'll do anything to get ahold of it. The web's growing rougher and rougher, so there's definitely danger brewing . . . and it looks to me like evil. Evil of the very nastiest kind." The Ancient One sounded very weary.

"But if we can find the egg before anyone else does," Gracie said soothingly, "surely it'll all be OK? Great-Uncle Alvin might even know where we should look. And then all we have to do is take it back to— Oh! Where ARE the dragons, Auntie Edna?"

"The dragons have always lived in the Seven-Mile Caves, far beyond the Wild Enchanted Forest. A long way away from here. And you're quite right, Gracie dear. That would solve the problem beautifully." Edna's one blue eye lit up. "The dragons would be thrilled if a Trueheart brought their son or daughter back to them. . . . They believe an egg is always influenced by the company it keeps just before hatching. Of course, the mother dragon always tries to be there, but sometimes that just isn't possible."

"So if someone nasty found it," Gracie wanted to know, "would the dragon be born evil?"

Edna sighed. "It would. And what's worse, whoever found it would be twice as bad themselves. The imminent birth of any new creature is always a time when the forces of good and evil gather strength, and unfortunately the evil ones are particularly skilled at harnessing this for their own hideous aims."

For a moment Gracie didn't say anything. "So it works both ways?" she said at last.

The Ancient One nodded, and Gracie gave her one of her beaming smiles. "That could be useful," she said, "because I really want to find that egg, and I really want to take it home to its parents. Marcus said he'd take me to see a flight of dragons for my birthday—maybe this is the perfect opportunity!"

"Spoken like the Trueheart you are, dearest girl." Edna stood up. "But we still don't know if we're making a fuss about nothing. Now, off you go to bed. You've got an early start in the morning."

Gracie kissed the Ancient One good night, but it took her a while to get to sleep. Although half of her was excited by the thought of an adventure, the other half was apprehensive. *Let's hope Great-Uncle Alvin has the answers,* she told herself. *And then if there is an egg, Marcus and I can go find it. I wonder if we'll be able to watch it hatch? I'd absolutely love to see a baby dragon.* And she finally closed her eyes.

It seemed no time at all before she was woken by Gubble banging loudly on her door. The door, offended at such rough treatment so early in the morning, slid swiftly up to the ceiling, and Gracie sighed. "Gubble!" she called. "You've upset the door again. Could you go downstairs and put the kettle on? I'll have to climb out of the window."

A loud grunt suggested that the troll had heard her, and Gracie got dressed as quickly as she could. "I do so wish I had my coat up here." She spoke out loud and did her best to sound plaintive, while keeping a hopeful eye on the ceiling. "It's going to be horribly wet climbing out of the window after all that rain—I'm going to get absolutely drenched." At once the door slid back into place with an apologetic *thud.* Gracie looked at it gratefully. "Thank you so much. I'm very sorry about Gubble. He doesn't know his own strength." The door opened wide in response, and Gracie hopped through before it could change its mind. She found herself at the top of a flight of stairs and saw Marcus at the bottom, looking baffled.

"I can't find the WATER WINGS door anywhere," he told her. "That is the kitchen, isn't it? I've been searching for ages. I keep finding myself in room seventeen with the looms, and your auntie Elsie's getting really tired of telling me which way to go."

"The whole house is a bit upset at the moment," Gracie said. "It's not a good sign. Did Auntie Elsie say how the web was looking?"

Marcus rubbed his nose. "She was too busy trying to stop your stepsister from messing up her patterns. What does the web of power do, exactly? I mean, I know it's kind of magic, but what's it for?"

Gracie made a quick sideways jump and caught hold of a door handle that was doing its best to sneak past unseen. As she led Marcus into the kitchen, she said, "I don't think even the crones know quite how the web works. It mustn't ever break—that I do know. I think it sort of holds good and evil in some kind of balance, if that makes any sense."

"Can it tell when something dangerous is about to happen?" Marcus wanted to know.

He sounded so hopeful that Gracie couldn't help smiling as she answered. "It changes all the time . . . and yes — it looks different when things are going wrong."

Marcus was delighted. "Your auntie Edna said it looked terrible yesterday. Come on! Let's have breakfast, and then we can get going."

Breakfast was soon disposed of, but while Marcus was outside saddling his pony, Gracie was presented with an unexpected problem. Gubble, it seemed, was convinced he was to be one of the party.

"But Gubble," Gracie explained, "it's only a visit to a bat. It's Marlon's great-uncle Alvin. We need to talk to him — that's all." Gubble grunted disagreement, and Gracie sighed. The last thing she wanted was to hurt his feelings, but he was not a speedy traveler. "Tell you what," she suggested. "Why don't you meet us at Wadingburn? We're going to see the professor after we've been to Fracture, and if you went there directly, we'd probably arrive about the same time." Gubble appeared to be wavering. "If things *do* happen to go wrong," Gracie went on, "there won't be any danger at Fracture — it'll be somewhere inside the Five

Kingdoms. And if we need you, I promise we'll send Alf to find you and tell you. And you know I always keep my promises."

There was a long thoughtful silence while Gubble's very small brain churned its way through Gracie's suggestions. At last he came to a conclusion. "Gracie still angry."

"Why would I be angry with you?" Gracie asked in surprise.

Gubble sighed. "Ate egg sandwiches."

"You ate the chocolate cake as well," Gracie said, and she hugged him. "No. I'm not angry. Heavens, no. So will you meet us at Wadingburn? In the library?"

There was a shorter silence, and then Gubble announced, "Niven's Knowe. Gubble go to Niven's Knowe."

Gracie smiled. "You've done it again, Gubble. I said 'Heavens, no,' not 'Niven's Knowe.' And we aren't going anywhere near there. Well . . ." She paused, and honesty made her add, "Not unless we find out there's a dragon's egg, and it's about to hatch. If that happens, then yes. We will be going to Niven's Knowe."

A mutinous expression settled over the troll's flat face. "Gubble go to Niven's Knowe."

"OK." Gracie gave up. "If that's what you want.

We'll come and collect you." She gave him another hug, and the two of them walked outside to find Marcus waiting, with Glee beside him. The path to the front gate was doing its best to shape itself into a heart, and Gracie looked around suspiciously. "Is Alf here, by any chance?"

"Present and correct!" A small shape whizzed around her head. "Are we ready, boys and girls? Are we steady? Oh! What's the troll doing?"

"He's going to Niven's Knowe," Gracie told him. "He—he's on a very special mission of his own. Aren't you, Gubble?"

Gubble nodded solemnly before stamping heavily on the end of the path. With a disappointed wriggle, it went back to its usual position, and Gubble stomped his way out through the gate. He made a sharp turn, then headed into the thickest of the bushes and began to follow his own particular version of a crow's flight to Niven's Knowe.

"Wow." Marcus sighed as he watched Gubble plow his way through the middle of an especially dense and prickly blackberry bush with no apparent problem. "Does anything ever stop him?"

"Not much," Gracie admitted. "Of course, he has to stop for a bit if his head falls off, but that doesn't seem to have happened much lately. And he's not too keen on rivers because he can't swim. He has to hold his breath and walk along the bottom. He can hold his breath for ages, though."

Gubble was now well out of sight, but his continued progress could be tracked by the sound of crashing branches. Alf, feeling that quite enough attention had been paid to the troll, flew down onto Marcus's shoulder. "Shouldn't we be on our way, Mr. Prince?"

"You're right," Marcus agreed. "Gracie, do you want to ride behind me? You're light. Glee won't mind. Later on we can walk for a bit so he doesn't get tired out."

Gracie gave Alf a warning glance as she swung herself up onto Glee's back, and he gazed up at the sky with the most innocent of expressions. "La-di-da," he sang. "La-di-da." Marcus touched Glee's sides with his heels, and they trotted through the gate and steadily down the faint track that led between the trees. Behind them the path outside the house gave a couple of twitches before forming itself into a perfect heart.

Chapter Twelve

Princess Fedora, much fortified by an evening with her mother, Queen Kesta of Dreghorn—and even more fortified by having had the forethought to pack herself a large picnic breakfast before leaving the comforts of her old home—was ready to hold her interviews. Her mother had promised a return visit in a day or two, and Fedora was determined to have everything in order by the time she arrived. She had put out her best gold pen and a pad of crisp white paper, sharpened several pencils, tied her hair back with an efficient and business-like clip, insisted on Tertius hauling a very heavy desk into the palace dining room, settled herself behind it, decided it was too big and made him exchange it for a smaller desk from her own rooms, loosened her hair again, and finally settled herself in position. *The Handbook of Palace Management* was prominently displayed beside her.

Tertius, still panting from his exertions, had gone for a walk. Fedora's picnic breakfast had been for one person only, and he was brooding heavily on her selfishness as he strode about the grounds. King Horace had been seen some while earlier making a beeline for Mrs. Basket's cottage, and Tertius longed to join him, but his loyalty to Fedora held him back. "Although it would jolly well serve her right if I had breakfast there," he muttered. "And if I don't get any lunch, I'm jolly well going to ask Mrs. Basket to come back to the palace. I'm going to take a stand; I really am. Father will back me up, and Feddy will just have to put up with it. So there." And he marched on, feeling unusually forceful and determined.

His young wife, equally determined to sort out the domestic affairs of the palace, rang the little bell on her desk. After rather too long a time for her liking, a somewhat flustered Saturday Mousewater appeared.

"You'll have to come quicker than that, Saturday," Fedora told her. "And where's your clean apron?"

Saturday bobbed a curtsy. "If you please, ma'am, I was a-making the beds before lighting the fires and washing the floors and tidying up in the kitchen when you did call."

"Oh." The princess gave a gracious nod. "I see.

Erm . . . yes. Very well. Could you ask the first applicants to come in, please? Ask them to form an orderly line, and remind them not to make too much noise while they're waiting."

Saturday's mouth opened and closed. "Applicants, miss — beg pardon — ma'am?"

Fedora began to tap on the desk with her gold pen. "The people who have come for the jobs, Saturday. The new maidservants. The cooks."

Saturday pushed her mobcap back on her head so she could scratch her ear. "If you please, ma'am, there ain't anyone."

"What? Are you sure? Isn't there *anybody* waiting out there?"

Fedora suddenly sounded very much younger, and Saturday, to her surprise, found herself feeling sorry for the princess. "There's nobody at all, miss. Was you expecting them all to be at the back door, like? Or might some have come to the front?"

"I suppose they might." Fedora put her pen down. "Maybe it's too early in the morning. What time do people usually come to interviews?"

Saturday bobbed another curtsy. "I'm sure as I can't really say, miss. But I'll go and have another look just in case I missed someone, like." She hurried away, leaving the young homemaker to have a quick check in her *Handbook*. Sadly, there was no entry entitled "What to do if nobody answers your advertisement."

I'm absolutely not *going to ask Mrs. Basket to come back,* Fedora told herself. *I suppose I don't mind if the footmen do . . . but not that horrid old woman.*

Saturday, meanwhile, was at the back door. In the distance she could just make out two skinny figures; they appeared to be slapping at each other rather than coming toward the palace, and she shut the door again. A quick peek out of the front door gave a better result. An enormous figure dressed all in white was—what *was* it doing? Saturday screwed up her eyes to try and make it out. The figure wasn't walking. It seemed to be . . . *billowing* was the only word Saturday could think of. Billowing up the drive. It was carrying a substantial carpetbag under one arm, and tucked under the other was the advertisement that Bobby had been sent to pin up in the marketplace. Sitting on one huge shoulder was a crow: balding, broken-feathered, and peering about with a greedy stare. Saturday, spellbound, waited on the doorstep.

As the figure came closer, it became clear that it was a woman, a woman easily as wide as she was tall. Not only was she dressed in white, but her face was

white—white with the pallid look and texture of well-kneaded dough. Her long, thin hair was also white, and when she turned her head and looked at Saturday from under white lashes, even her eyes appeared to have no color.

"I've come to cook." The woman's oddly monotonous voice sounded as if she had stolen it from someone else and was not yet used to it. "Where is the kitchen?"

Saturday swallowed hard. Every bit of her wanted to run away and hide in a cupboard until this woman and her hideous bird had gone, but she forced herself to say, "If you please, ma'am, Princess Fedora is in the dining room. She be interviewing there, like. If you tells me your name, I'll let her know you're here."

"Tell her she'll find Mercy Grinder in the kitchen," the woman said. "I am answering her advertisement for a cook." The parchment was waved in front of Saturday's nose. "Now, show me the way."

Saturday looked around to see if Bobby was anywhere in sight, but there was no sign of him.

Mercy Grinder, with all the assurance of a large ship under full sail, moved herself and her luggage into the hallway with a smoothness that made Saturday wonder if she was on wheels rather than legs. "Show me the way," Mercy repeated. "Show me—"

"Follow me, ma'am." Saturday gave up. She was only too well aware that Princess Fedora would be angry, but Mercy Grinder was as impossible to argue with as a mountain. "Follow me." Saturday set off through a maze of marble corridors, finally arriving at a green-baize door. Opening this, she pointed to the flight of stairs that led down to the butler's pantry, the storerooms, and the kitchen. "The kitchen's at the bottom."

"What do they like to eat?"

Saturday was a nervous girl; she found it all too easy to imagine creaking doors and rustles in the darkness hiding ghouls and ghosties that might spring out on her. Mercy Grinder's voice was the opposite of scary in that it had the same regular metallic quality as the tick of the grandfather clock in the hall, but nevertheless cold shivers ran up and down Saturday's spine as she tried to find an answer. "Erm . . ." Her thoughts circled wildly. "Erm . . . the princess is very fond of chocolate cake. With chocolate-cream icing."

"Chocolate cake. I will make chocolate cake with chocolate-cream icing." And Mercy Grinder descended the stairs without appearing to touch a single step.

For the first time since she had come to the palace, Saturday Mousewater wondered about running away. If she had not had a proud mother who thought she was the luckiest girl in the world to live in a palace, she might have given in to the urge. As it was, she took a deep breath and went to tell Fedora that she, Saturday Mousewater, the most unimportant person in the palace, had inadvertently employed a cook. What was worse, she was a cook who had the most unpleasant and disreputable-looking bird Saturday had ever seen as a pet.

As she approached the dining room, her heart thumping and her knees trembling, Saturday met Bobby coming out. "Did you see them?" he whispered, his eyes wide. "It's those twins—the ones I saw before! They were knocking on the back door, and I've just brought them in, and they look weirder than ever! And they want to come and work here!"

Saturday, relieved to be saved from certain dismissal for another few minutes, looked doubtful. "Surely 'tisn't possible. The princess is that fussy—she'll not take anyone if they be weird, like."

Bobby winked at her, then bent down so his eye was level with the keyhole. "I can see them in there!" he reported. "Princess F. is reading them a list of what they've got to do! That'll be from that book of hers . . . sounds like there's pages 'n' pages of it. Oh!" An expression of intense excitement came over his face, and he watched carefully for several seconds before standing up and shaking his head in astonishment. "Blow me down and blow me over!"

"What is it?" Saturday asked. "Tell me! What is it?"

"Prince T. He must have come in through the other door." Bobby rubbed his eyes. "Shaking his head and looking cross as two sticks, he was, so guess what? She gets all uppity doo-dah and tells them——" Bobby came to an abrupt stop, grabbed Saturday's hand, and dragged her into hiding behind a substantial marble column. "Shh!" he whispered in her ear. "They're coming!"

Saturday held her breath as the dining-room door opened and the twins came sailing out. Smirking, they gave each other a thumbs-up.

"Easy-peasy!" Conducta boasted.

Globula held up the princess's gold pen. "And look what I've got!" Conducta fished under her skirt and produced Fedora's diamond hair clip. "Like taking candy from a kid!"

Bobby and Saturday watched openmouthed as the twins hopped and skipped their way to the back door and slammed it shut behind them.

Chapter Thirteen

Professor Scallio was tidying up the library, and Marlon was keeping him company. The professor had benefited from a good night's sleep and was feeling much more positive; Marlon, on the other hand, was stiff after his long flights and decidedly cranky.

"Marcus and Gracie should be here by teatime, with any luck," the professor said as he heaved a pile of books off the floor and onto the table he used as a desk. "And hopefully they'll bring us good news."

"Or bad." Marlon yawned. "And that's supposing old Unc actually knows anything."

"What?" The professor paused, book in hand. "I thought he knew all there was to know about dragons."

Marlon stretched his wings and winced. "So he says. Of course, he could be fibbing."

Professor Scallio put his book down. "Marlon, what do you mean? Have we sent Gracie and Marcus off on a wild-goose chase?"

"Nah." The bat shrugged, then sniggered. "Don't you mean wild-dragon chase?"

"This isn't a joke, Marlon." The professor pulled his handkerchief out of his pocket and wiped his forehead. "Oh dear, oh dear. There haven't been any reports of sightings since yesterday morning; I'd almost convinced myself everything was going to be all right. But now you tell me Great-Uncle Alvin is unreliable! I wonder if I should go see the Ancient One. But I suspect she doesn't know any more than we do . . . oh dearie, dearie me!"

Marlon realized he had gone too far. "Sorry, Prof. Didn't mean to upset you. Old war wounds playing up a bit, dontcha know. No worries—no worries at all. Great-Uncle Alvin'll put them straight. Born above the dragon lofts, he was—he and all his brothers and sisters. Dragons in the blood, you could say." He coughed. "You've missed a book, by the way."

The professor inspected his informant somewhat doubtfully. Marlon was not above twisting the truth if he felt it was convenient, but on this occasion he sounded genuine. "Well, I hope you're right. Now, what was that about my missing one?"

Marlon waved a wing. "Down there. Under the table."

Professor Scallio bent to see where Marlon was pointing, then straightened again. "That one's propping up the table leg. The floor's uneven, and there's nothing I hate more than writing on a wobbly table . . . oh. Oh, I wonder . . . no. That would be too much of a coincidence . . . wouldn't it?" With some difficulty, he bent down and pulled out the book.

It was old and very dirty; the housemaids who occasionally swirled a damp mop around the library floor had paid it no attention. The professor laid it carefully on the table, then gave it a quick wipe with his hanky before opening it. Dust flew everywhere, and Marlon and the professor both sneezed loudly.

"Let's see. . . ." Professor Scallio turned the ancient crackling pages. "No. No, it's a book of accounts. Accounts for the palace of Niven's Knowe. Wonder how it came to be here. It's quite old, but not what I was looking for. Not at all."

Marlon was looking over the professor's shoulder. "Hang on, Prof. Don't put it back yet. How old is it?"

"Let me see . . ." There was a pause. "Refers back maybe fifty . . . no, more like sixty or seventy years ago. Difficult to say exactly because most of the entries are dated only by month, but there's a bill for a carriage wheel for King Huzzell, and he's King Horace's grandfather . . . oh, my word! I don't believe it! Here's a date! They're the accounts for eighty years ago! Marlon, you're a genius!"

Marlon folded his wings in a nonchalant manner. "Modesty's my middle name. All part of the service."

Professor Scallio didn't hear. He was eagerly turning page after page, muttering as he did so. "'Sheets . . . chickens . . . county ball . . . christening party . . . three silver forks and a carving knife' . . . Fascinating stuff, this, really fascinating. Why do you think they needed a bowl of frogs and twenty yards of thick green velvet?"

Marlon shrugged. Social history was not one of his interests. "Any mention of dragons, Prof?"

"Dragons? Oh, yes. Let's see." The professor was glowing with enthusiasm. "Well, I never! Listen to this, Marlon! 'Payment to Mrs. Grettishaw in compensation for fire damage to three lines of personal washing and the destruction of a newly planted beech hedge.' That must have been caused by the dragons, don't you think? And look . . . here's more. Haystacks burned to the ground . . . schoolhouse roof singed . . . smoke damage to a cartload of apples . . ." More pages were turned, the professor murmuring happily, and then—"*Aha!* 'Five bales of finest nesting straw for dragons!' NESTING STRAW!" Professor Scallio leaped to his feet and did a dance right around the table and back again. "There we are! Conclusive proof! There were dragons in Niven's Knowe eighty years ago, and at least one of them was nesting!"

Marlon coughed. "Erm . . . hate to pour cold water 'n' all that, but aren't you forgetting something?"

The professor stopped mid-prance. "Eh?"

"'Scuse me if I'm wrong," Marlon said slowly, "but doesn't a nest mean an egg? And doesn't an egg mean a baby dragon? And isn't that what the evil guys and gals out there want more than anything?"

The professor stared, gulped, rubbed his head, and collapsed into a chair. "You're right," he said dully. "You're absolutely right. How could I have forgotten?"

Marlon flew up to a shelf. The news that had made the professor despair was acting on him like a tonic. "Don't you worry! Leave it to me, Prof. Never fear, Marlon's here. . . . Be back in five—*ciao!*" And he was gone.

Chapter Fourteen

If Tertius had not chosen that precise moment to come back from his walk, Fedora would never have employed the twins. Just being in the same room with them made her feel uncomfortable. Admittedly, they had claimed to be able to perform every single one of the tasks listed in the palace *Handbook,* but their shifty eyes and sly smiles were not at all engaging. She suggested a ridiculously low salary in the hope that they would throw up their hands in horror and leave immediately, but instead they nodded and said it was quite acceptable. Fedora furtively turned over a page of the *Handbook.* "When an applicant is to be rejected, no reasons or excuses are necessary. Merely state that the post has been offered to a more suitable candidate and dismiss the applicant with a polite but firm refusal." Fedora sucked the end of her pen and pretended to be studying her notes. What should she do? Her mother was due for a visit, and she had told King Horace she would have everything sorted out by the end of the day. On the other hand, there was something in the way the twins were staring at her that made her feel decidedly nervous.

No. Fedora made up her mind: the twins would not do. She took a deep breath and looked up, fully intending to deliver her best attempt at a "polite but firm refusal," but was distracted by the sight of Tertius signaling from the far end of the dining room. He was pointing at the twins and shaking his head, and as he hurried to Fedora's side, he made the fatal mistake of frowning at her.

That's so mean of Terty, Fedora thought as she turned away from him. *Here I am, working my fingers to the bone trying to sort out his horrid palace affairs, and he's not even trying to help.* She gave the twins the benefit of her most gracious smile. "Conducta and Globula, I'm delighted to tell you that you have been successful."

"Hang on a minute!" Tertius, still frowning, took her arm. "Can I have a word, Feddy?"

Fedora's smile became fixed. "Of course, dearest one. Poppet. Sugar chops. But first I'd like you to meet our two new housemaids. This is Conducta, and this is Globula. No. This is Globula, and this is Conducta . . .

at least . . ." Fedora hesitated, but the twins offered no help. She went on quickly, "And I'm sure they'll be quite wonderful, and they'll start work just as soon as they can. Perhaps"— she looked inquiringly at her two new employees—"perhaps this afternoon? After lunch?"

"OK, miss." Conducta did not sound enthusiastic.

"See you later," Globula agreed.

Both twins gave Tertius a triumphant glare before marching away. As the door closed behind them, the prince sank into a chair. "Honestly, Feddy! What on earth are you playing at? We can't possibly have those girls here. They give me the creeps!"

Fedora bridled. "I've told them they can come, so you're too late. They can do absolutely everything on the list in my handbook, and they've agreed to a really tiny wage, so I think you should be congratulating me, not telling me off."

Tertius slumped further. "Whatever will Father say? He's sure to want to know whether you asked them for references, and I bet you jolly well didn't."

There was a pause while Fedora arranged her pencils in a complicated pattern. "Oh. Erm. That is, not exactly. I . . . I sort of forgot about references. But I'm sure they'll be fine." Aware she had made a mistake, she changed her approach. "Darling lovely gorgeous beautiful Terty, don't be cross with your silly-billy Feddy!" She jumped up from her desk and wrapped her arms around the prince's neck. "Feddy was only trying to be a good girl and make you happy!"

Tertius gave in and shortly afterward found himself apologizing for criticizing his wife's amazing interviewing skills.

Fedora forgave him with a kiss on the end of his nose, and peace was restored. "Shall I bring you a lovely cup of tea?" she suggested.

This reminded Tertius of his lack of breakfast. Disentangling himself from his beloved, he asked, "I don't suppose you've found a cook, have you?"

Fedora was saved from having to reply by a tentative knock on the door. "Come in!" she called—and Saturday, anxiously twisting her duster around and around her fingers, came slowly into the room.

"If you please, miss," she began, "there's something I needs to tell you, like . . ." She stopped, quite unable to think of a way to explain Mercy Grinder's arrival. "You see, miss . . . I means, ma'am . . . that is . . ."

But Fedora wasn't listening. Neither was Tertius. They were both sniffing the air. The unmistakable smell of rich dark chocolate cake was floating along the corridor, and the prince let out a wild whoop of joy. "It's

Mrs. Basket! Darling, *darling* Feddy—you've asked her back!" And he set off at a run along the corridors and down the stairs to the kitchen. "Mrs. B.!" he gasped as he hurtled around the kitchen door—and froze.

"Chocolate cake," said Mercy Grinder as she swirled chocolate cream inches thick. "I've made chocolate cake."

Tertius was a true prince of the Five Kingdoms. It took him only seconds to recover his composure and remember his manners. Stiffly he bowed. "Madam. I'm delighted to make your acquaintance. I presume you are the new cook. Welcome to the palace of Niven's Knowe."

Fedora, following behind him, hardly noticed the enormous white shape on the other side of the kitchen table. She was staring at the miracle that was the cake. "That looks utterly amazing!" she said breathlessly. "Can I have some right now this minute?"

Mercy picked up a knife and cut the princess a more than generous slice.

"Oooooh." Fedora sighed in rapture. "Do try this, Terty. It's . . . it's magic."

"I'm sure it's excellent." Tertius was still recovering from his shock at finding Mrs. Basket's place in the kitchen taken by someone who looked so very large and

so very pale, and so very unlike any cook he had ever seen before. "Almost as good as Mrs. Basket's. Well done." Then, noticing Fedora's rapturous expression and the undoubted quality of the cake, he began to see there might be advantages in the situation. "Erm . . . I don't suppose there's any chance of a cooked breakfast? Eggs and bacon and mushrooms . . . that kind of thing? Toast? Marmalade?"

"Eggs and bacon and mushrooms," Mercy repeated in her monotonous voice, and she left the cake and made her way over to the stove. "Toast and marmalade." As Mercy picked up the frying pan, Saturday crept cautiously around the door. She looked nervously at Fedora, but the princess was helping herself to a second slice of cake with a blissful smile on her face.

"Ah! Saturday! Could you bring me up my breakfast when it's ready, please?" Tertius beamed at her. "I'll be in the dining room. Feddy, darling . . . I don't think you should eat all that cake at once. Why don't you leave some for Father?"

Fedora looked up as Tertius left the kitchen, a glazed expression in her eyes. "Why shouldn't I eat it all?" she said thickly. "Itsh the beshtish cake I've ever eaten." And she cut another slice.

Standing at the stove with the frying pan in her hand, Mercy Grinder gave a small satisfied nod. Carrion, perched on the top of the dresser and hidden from sight by a large soup tureen, opened his beak wide in a silent laugh. Saturday Mousewater, watching openmouthed from the doorway, felt a cold chill settle in the pit of her stomach.

Chapter Fifteen

Alf, baffled by Gracie's rejection of his romantic efforts on her behalf, had decided she must be suffering from shyness and took it upon himself to encourage her to talk to Marcus. To this end, he had been asking a stream of questions ever since leaving the House of the Ancient Crones.

"So, Mr. Prince, is it fun in your palace? What's it like having a twin brother? Miss Gracie's only got a stepsister, so she must be ever so lonely sometimes—isn't that right, Miss Gracie? But having a friend who's a little bit special must make ever such a difference—"

"Alf!" Marcus, who was beginning to get a headache from the nonstop twittering in his ear, pulled Glee to a sudden halt. "I've just had the most brilliant idea. Why don't you fly on ahead and check that Great-Uncle Alvin's in his cave?"

Alf looked doubtful, but Gracie clapped her hands. "Oh, that would be so helpful. You could tell him we're coming, and that I'm really looking forward to seeing him again."

"OK." Alf flew up and circled over their heads. "If you say so, Miss Gracie. I'll be as quick as I can. There and back in two ticks!"

Gracie began to say that there was no need for him to come back and he could wait for them at Uncle Alvin's, but she was too late. The little bat had gone.

"Phew!" Marcus heaved a sigh of relief. "I thought he was going to chatter all the way. How much farther have we got to go, would you say?"

Gracie glanced about her. "Maybe an hour or two's ride. And we don't have to go as far as Fracture itself, thank goodness."

Marcus, who knew about Gracie's unhappy childhood in the village, gave her knee a sympathetic pat. Gracie giggled, and he looked around in surprise. "What is it?"

"I was thinking of Alf." Gracie chortled, quite unable to stop laughing now that she had started. "If he'd seen you do that, he'd have had a seizure. . . . Oh, he is so funny!"

Marcus was silent while he considered. Was Alf funny?

He still felt strangely dithery every time he remembered how the little bat had told him to kiss Gracie. He'd even wondered once or twice if kissing her might not, in fact, be rather nice, but each time a dreadful picture of Arioso drooping over Nina-Rose had flashed up in his mind and he'd put the thought firmly away. He and Gracie were friends. Very good friends, but that was all. Absolutely all. It was true that if he had to go on an adventure, he'd much rather go with Gracie than with anyone else—there was no doubt about that—but that was different. So yes, Alf was funny. Marcus began to laugh, and he and Gracie rode on comfortably together until Alf came zooming back.

"Unc says he's not in for me, but he is for you, Miss Gracie. And he'll say hello to Mr. Prince if he has to, but please remember that he doesn't do bowing or charm."

Gracie grinned. "We'll be there soon. At least, we will if he hasn't moved—is he still in the same place?"

"Sure is. Crack in the rock. Which reminds me. I was wondering—"

"Shut it, kid." Marlon had flown silently down behind Alf. "Too much gab-gab-gabbing."

"WOW! Didn't see you, Uncle Marlon! Super glide or what! Cool! How do you do that?"

Marlon, briefly distracted, looked smug. "Trade

secret, kid. Trade secret. But I've got news." He settled on Gracie's shoulder and lowered his voice. "The prof's made a discovery. There was a nest. A dragon's nest. Niven's Knowe, eighty years ago. And you know what? In my book, nest equals egg."

"*Wheeeeeeeeeee!*" Alf let out an excited squeak and looped an ecstatic loop. "An egg! Where is it? When's it going to hatch? Yipp— OUCH! That hurt, Unc!" He rubbed his ear as he took himself off to a nearby twig.

"Good," Marlon said. "Top secret, right? Not a peep. Lips sealed. Mouth zipped. Get it?"

Alf, wide-eyed, nodded. "Got it."

Marcus, suppressing his excitement only a little more successfully than Alf, asked, "How did he find out?"

"Book of accounts for Niven's Knowe." Marlon was enjoying his moment of drama. "Record of nesting straw for dragons!"

"Was there any other information?" Gracie wanted to know.

Marlon shook his head. "*Nada.* Nothing."

"We'd better get to Niven's Knowe as fast as we can!" Marcus was alight with the thought of action. "We've absolutely got to find the egg before anyone else does. Tell you what: we'll go via Gorebreath, and we'll borrow Arry's pony so we can travel faster—"

Gracie put a gently restraining hand over his, saw Alf's beady eyes on her, and took it off again. "Actually, I think we should still go and see Great-Uncle Alvin. We need to know how old the dragon was, and if the egg's likely to be hatching soon . . . and he might even know where we should start looking."

"Good thinking, kiddo," Marlon said approvingly.

"Do you really think so?" Marcus looked crestfallen.

Gracie nodded, and the prince swallowed a sigh. "OK, then. But we'd better get going."

"I'll lead the way!" Alf flew a speedy zigzag under Glee's nose. "Come on, Mr. Prince! Follow me!"

"Hooray!" Marcus set off after Alf at a gallop; Gracie shut her eyes and held on tight.

It was only another twenty minutes before the rocky slopes that lay below the village of Fracture came into view, and Marcus pulled the pony back to a gentle walk, much to Gracie's relief.

"Good work!" Alf squeaked. "Here we are! Third crack in the rocks on the right."

Gracie slid off Glee's back, wondering if her knees were as wobbly as she thought they were. "Shall I go first?" she asked, but she was too late; Alf had already disappeared.

A second later he was out again, looking dazed and flying erratically. "He boxed my ears," he complained. "Everyone's doing it today. My head hurts." And he made a shaky landing on the back of Glee's saddle.

"Like I told you, kiddo," Marlon said with a distinct lack of sympathy. "Gab-gab-gab. Get what you ask for if you go on like that."

Gracie gave Alf a comforting stroke with her finger. "Cheer up," she told him. "I'll be back in a minute, and then if we do need to go to Niven's Knowe, you can show us the quickest way. I mean," she added hastily, "the easiest way."

She could hear Marlon laughing as she made her way between the rocks toward Great-Uncle Alvin's small, dark entrance, and found herself hoping the next stage of their adventure would be a little less uncomfortable. *It's OK for Marlon,* she thought. *He can fly. Oh, well—maybe I'll get better at riding if I have more practice.*

She was interrupted in her thoughts by a suspicious voice. "Is that you, Trueheart?"

Gracie nodded, realized she couldn't be seen, and made her way farther into the darkness. "That's right. How are you, Great-Uncle Alvin?"

"Still alive. Just. On your own, I hope?"

The voice was not welcoming, but Gracie smiled as she answered. "Quite on my own . . . Well, I came here with Marcus and Alf and Marlon, but they're waiting on the path."

There was a loud despising sniff. "Waste of space, those two. Don't know why you have anything to do with them, nice girl like you. Well? What can I do for you? I don't suppose you came here for the pleasure of my company. Nobody ever does."

"I came because you might have some very important information," Gracie told him. "In fact, you might be able to save the Five Kingdoms from a terrible danger."

The only response to this was another sniff.

"Come on, Great-Uncle Alvin," Gracie coaxed. "You know I'm a Trueheart. I don't tell lies. Just imagine what the Ancient Crones would do to me if I did."

"Hmph." The ancient bat fluttered down to Gracie's shoulder. "I'll believe you. Thousands wouldn't. So what was it you wanted to know?"

"It's about the dragons of Niven's Knowe," Gracie began—but she got no further.

Great-Uncle Alvin began a furious muttering that Gracie could hardly understand; she caught the words "humiliated" and "disgraced" but little else. At last the

muttering died away, leaving Alvin puffing and panting as if he'd flown an enormous distance.

"I'm so sorry," Gracie said. "I really am. If I'd known I was going to upset you so much, I'd never have come. P'raps I'd better go. . . . I'm sure we can find out about the egg some other way."

"What? What was that?" The bat sidled closer to Gracie's ear. "Did you say . . . egg? Do you mean . . . a dragon's egg?"

Gracie nodded. "That's right. Professor Scallio thinks there's a dragon's egg hidden somewhere in Niven's Knowe . . . And there are dragons flying around outside the borders—a golden one, a blue one, and a green one."

"The dragons of Niven's Knowe!" Great-Uncle Alvin's voice trembled. He flew down to Gracie's shoulder, and his soft fur tickled her cheek. "Lumiere, Indigo, and Luskentyre. They've come back. Come back at last, after all these years. And Lumiere is looking for her egg. . . . Of course she is." He took a deep breath and let it out in a long, satisfied sigh. "So . . . I was right. They chucked me out, but I was right all the time. Ha! And HA! And ha-ha-HA!" Great-Uncle Alvin began to stamp a small triumphant march up and down by Gracie's ear. "Where's that horrible nephew of mine?

Just wait till I tell him! Not that he's his father, of course, but I can still tell him I was right! Come on, Trueheart! I've got a score to settle!"

Gracie, perplexed by the bat's outburst but pleased he was so delighted, made her way to the cave entrance as quickly as she could and found herself blinking in the sunshine.

Alvin, still on her shoulder, raised himself to his full height and looked around for Marlon. "Where are you?" he squeaked. "Marlon Batster! Come here this minute!"

There was a flutter of wings, and Marlon and Alf appeared, closely followed by Marcus. "Did he . . . ?" Marcus asked, but Gracie put her finger to her lips.

"Listen to me!" The elderly bat spread his wings wide. "Listen to me! I was right! I was right! Driven out of the Five Kingdoms, taunted, told I was a fool — and all the time *I was right!*"

Marlon settled himself on a rock and stared at his great-uncle. "Old bat's gone batty," he observed in an undertone. "Lost it completely."

Alf hopped up and down on one leg. "Batty batty."

"Shh," Marcus whispered. "Let him have his say."

Great-Uncle Alvin glared at his relatives. "You, Marlon Batster and Alf Batster, don't know anything.

I was a respected bat once." He gave Alf an especially chilly look, even though the little bat had not made a sound. "It's true. The dragons of Niven's Knowe trusted me. Lumiere, Indigo, and Luskentyre. They were my friends. The dragon boy relied on me. We were mates. But one day a fire broke out in the market hall, and who was blamed? The dragons. And humans — begging your pardon, Trueheart — get overexcited. They marched to the palace with axes and rakes and pitchforks, and the king gave in to them. The dragons were rounded up and driven away, even though Lumiere was known to be nesting. Any one of them could have turned and avenged themselves, but they didn't. They went with dignity. It was a terrible day. Terrible."

Alvin paused to take a rasping breath, and Gracie looked at him anxiously as he went on. "As the dragons left, I noticed something odd. Lumiere was dragging behind the others and looking over her shoulder. 'That dragon's laid her egg,' I said — but nobody believed me. The dragon boy would have known I was right, but I couldn't find him. He'd been threatened by the mob, and he'd run away. The other bats laughed; when I went looking for the egg, they laughed even more. Your father, Marlon, laughed louder than anyone, and in the end I left the Five Kingdoms, but now"—

Great-Uncle Alvin's rusty creak of a voice strengthened with pride—"now you see I was right! You've found the egg, in the nick of time. Eighty years on. It'll be hatching any moment. Where was it? Where is it now?"

Gracie went pale, and Marcus looked stricken. Even Alf was struck dumb. It was Marlon who said, "Sorry, Unc. We don't know."

"You don't know? Then why are you here? We must find it! We must find it at once!" Alvin flapped his faded wings, staggered, gasped, and fell over in a small crumpled heap.

"Is he dead?" Alf asked in hushed tones.

"Nah. Tough as old boots, that one. Well . . . so my dad said." Marlon did not sound convinced.

Gracie, who was cradling the elderly bat in her hands, shook her head. "I think he's just old and exhausted. Maybe I ought to take him to the Ancient Crones."

"But we can't! There isn't time!" Marcus was certain they should delay no longer. "Couldn't we take him with us?"

Gracie looked down at the limp bundle of leathery wings and fur and bit her lip. "I don't know. Maybe."

"'Scuse me, but if we're going to find the dragon's egg, Great-Uncle Alvin'll be mad if he doesn't see the action," Alf piped up.

There was a feeble stirring in Gracie's hands. "More sense to that boy than I thought," said a faint voice.

Everyone sighed with relief. "Like I said. Tough as old boots." Marlon gave his great-uncle an encouraging wings-up, and Marcus pulled out a handkerchief and made a soft bed in his saddlebag.

"Can you see all right from there?" Gracie asked tenderly as she tucked Alvin in.

"See?" The voice was now querulous, and Gracie and Marcus grinned. Great-Uncle Alvin was obviously recovering fast. "What would I want to see? I'm going to sleep. Wake me up the second we get to Niven's Knowe. Don't forget." A moment later a series of minute snores suggested that the bat was as good as his word.

"Right!" Marcus swung himself onto Glee's back and held out a stirrup so Gracie could climb up behind him. "Let's go!"

"We'll need to go slower than before," Gracie pointed out. "We don't want to hurt Great-Uncle Alvin, and we absolutely mustn't draw attention to ourselves. Remember we've got to find the egg before anybody else does!"

"Oh. Yes. I suppose so," Marcus agreed, but as Glee set off down the track that led to Gorebreath and beyond, he made sure the pony was moving at a swift trot.

Chapter Sixteen

King Horace was deep in thought. He had been fed a rather less than substantial breakfast at Mrs. Basket's cottage, and it had been made very clear that he could not expect to continue to dine at that good lady's expense unless she was formally reinstated as palace cook. Mr. Trout—sitting in front of a plate piled high with eggs, mushrooms, bacon, beans, tomatoes, fried bread, and fried potatoes—had supported Mrs. Basket's point of view, but with rather more deference and the offer of a couple of mushrooms. The footmen were too busy playing cards in a corner to make any remark, and the housemaids and pages were nowhere to be seen. King Horace could only presume they had gone home to their respective families.

Hmph, the king said to himself as he wandered back across the park. *Wonder if Bluebell's had any ideas about cooks? Might call on her.* He pulled his watch out of his pocket and consulted it. *Not far off till lunchtime. I'll pop home and see how the two young 'uns are doing, and then I'll take the carriage and go to Wadingburn. Unless the coachman's gone as well, of course. Better go around by the stables and check.*

His visit to the stables was reassuring, and King Horace made his way into the palace. To his amazement, he was greeted by a delicious smell of roast chicken and potatoes, and his eyes shone as he hurried toward the dining room. He burst through the door and found Tertius and Fedora sitting at the table, and in between them was the most astonishing array of food laid out on a snow-white cloth.

"Well, well, well!" The king rubbed his hands together as he settled himself beside Tertius and beamed at Fedora. "You've found us a cook, and a very good one, too, by the look of things. What a clever little thing you are!"

Fedora smiled a slow lazy smile, and King Horace jumped. *She looks . . . fat!* he thought. *But how can that be? I saw her only this morning!* He turned to Tertius and saw that he, too, had a puffy look about him.

"Food's fantastic," the prince drawled. "Help yourself, Daddy-o. After this we've ordered lots 'n' lots of

different desserts . . . and we're going to gobble them all, aren't we, my cuddly-wuddly-duddly princess?"

Odd, thought the king. *Very odd, indeed.* He leaned forward and absently helped himself to a large plateful. "Don't suppose you've had a chance to find a butler yet? Or any footmen?"

"Who cares . . . 's long as we've got desserts." Tertius stuck a fork in what was left of the chicken and waved it above his head. "'Ray for Mer . . . Mer . . ."

"Mershy Grinder." Fedora nodded enthusiastically before toppling forward, her head in her plate.

"Oh, my goodness!" King Horace leaped to his feet. "Is she all right?"

Tertius tossed the chicken away. "Little diddums is fine. Eat your din-dins, Daddy-o, and don't be a fussy-wussy ol' fusspot."

King Horace frowned. Something was wrong. Very wrong . . . but he had no idea what it was or how to deal with it. Fedora had begun to snore, so she was evidently not exactly ill—but Tertius? He had never spoken to his father like that before. The king rubbed his hair until it stood straight up on end and, while he was thinking, took a mouthful of crispy roast potato. At once a strange peacefulness wrapped around him. He took another mouthful and wondered what he had been worrying about. All was well. All was very, very well . . . and as he continued to eat, his cares fell away, until all he could think of was the entrancing crunchiness of the carrots, the sweetness of the peas, and the delicious creaminess of the cauliflower.

Down in the kitchen, Mercy Grinder was filling dishes with chocolate mousse, lemon sponge, apple pie, strawberry cheesecake . . . all the requested desserts. Saturday Mousewater's arms were already aching from carrying heavy trays; Bobby, who had helped himself to several spoonfuls of cherry trifle when nobody was looking, was sitting in front of the fire with a dreamy smile on his face, ignoring requests for help. With a weary sigh, Saturday picked up yet another tray and set off for the stairs. When she reached the top, she began the long walk to the dining room; on arrival she found the three members of the royal family sprawled in their chairs, fast asleep.

"Ah . . . erm . . . ahem?" Saturday coughed as politely as she could, but there was not so much as a twitch in reply. With another sigh, she placed the dessert dishes on the sideboard and began to clear away the dirty plates and half-empty bowls of vegetables. A carrot slice fell on the tablecloth, and without thinking, she picked it up and put it in her mouth. "YEUCH!" The taste was astonishingly horrible; her tongue curled, then burned as if she had eaten a handful of peppercorns. It tasted like a panful of ashes swept from a dirty fireplace. Saturday gulped down first one glass of water and then another. Eyeing the other vegetables with suspicion, she tried a minute sliver of cheese. This was almost worse, and she rubbed furiously at her mouth with the back of her hand before drinking more water. Was *none* of it edible? Dumping the dirty dishes in a pile, she picked up a teaspoon and investigated the chocolate mousse. This time her nose began to tingle, and she sneezed several times in quick succession.

Fedora rolled her head off her plate and looked up, her eyes bleary. "Don't feel well," she said. "Feel . . . feel dizzy. Ever so dizzy. Whirly-whirly-whirly-woo . . . and hungry. Ever so hungry . . ."

"I'll put the desserts out at once, miss," Saturday said quickly.

The princess pulled herself up with an effort and stood swaying by her chair. She had intended to help herself to a generous portion of strawberry cheesecake, but her eye was caught by *The Handbook of Palace Management* lying beside her plate. It had fallen open at the title page, and the formidable author was directing a strongly disapproving gaze straight at Fedora. Underneath were the words "Moderation in all things must be your watchword. There is no room in a well-run palace for self-indulgence of *any* kind. An example must always be set." Fedora gulped and sank back on her chair. Her mouth was watering and her stomach was insisting it needed cheesecake, but . . . She swallowed hard and shut her eyes. *An example must always be set.*

Saturday gave her employer an anxious glance. "Would you like some water, miss?"

"Yesh . . . I mean, yes, please." Fedora opened her eyes again and saw the sleeping Tertius and King Horace. "What's been going on?"

"You've been eating your dinner, like," Saturday said. She poured a glass of water and handed it to the princess. "Maybe something didn't agree with you, miss."

Fedora drank the water and held out the glass for more. Three glasses later she was looking and feeling more normal. "Why are there so many desserts?" she asked in tetchy tones. "I'm sure I never ordered as many as that."

"If you please, miss, they was all asked for. You

and the prince chose them. And His Majesty, like. His Majesty wanted the apple pie 'n' the sponge cake 'n' the rice pudding—"

"That's enough!" Fedora held up her hand. A sudden suspicion floated into her mind, and she asked, somewhat tentatively, "Saturday . . . have the king and the prince been drinking?"

Saturday looked shocked. "Oh, no, miss. Nothing like that."

Fedora sat up straighter. "No. Of course, I didn't think for a moment that they had. Clear all this away, Saturday. We won't be wanting much tonight. Perhaps a couple of boiled eggs each."

"Certainly, miss. I'll tell Mrs. Grinder." Saturday bobbed a curtsy and went back to clearing the table.

The princess picked up her handbook, stood up, and then sat down again. The mention of Mercy Grinder had reminded her of an unanswered question . . . but what was it? Try as she would, the memory kept escaping. She shut her eyes again, and all of a sudden it was there. Was it Queen Bluebell who had sent Mercy Grinder to the palace? Or had King Horace appointed her? Was she—Fedora frowned at the thought—a friend of Mrs. Basket? Or had she simply appeared . . . in which case the rules in the *Handbook* had been severely violated. She began to shake Tertius. "Tertius! Wake up! Wake up this minute!"

There was no response. Fedora's shaking became more frenzied.

"I think he's down for the count, miss," Saturday offered.

Fedora, quite unaware that she had gravy in her hair and a jaunty piece of broccoli tucked behind one ear, put on her most superior expression. "Don't gawp, girl. Kindly get on with clearing everything away. It must be getting late. . . . Oh! That reminds me. Have the two new housemaids arrived? I asked them to come this afternoon."

Saturday had been doing her best to forget about Conducta and Globula. She shook her head. "No, miss. There don't be no sign of them."

"Tell them to report to me as soon as they get here," Fedora ordered, "and then they can go down to the kitchen. I'll be in the upstairs sitting room. Now, take those dishes away."

Saturday bobbed another curtsy, picked up a tray, and departed.

Fedora waited until the door had closed before bursting into tears and throwing herself on Tertius in a storm of weeping. "Terty! TERTY! Wake up!

There's something weird going on and I want to ask you something and I need you to wake up right NOW!" As her husband took no notice, she picked up a jug of iced lemonade and poured it over him. "Wake up!" she screamed. "WAKE UP!"

It was King Horace who raised his head. "What's all the noise about?" he inquired. "Devil of a rumpus goin' on! My apple pie here yet? I'm starving!"

Chapter Seventeen

The twins were making their way slowly back to the palace. It was nearly four o'clock; they had decided to take Fedora's instruction of "after lunch" as a general suggestion rather than an order and had gone home for several large helpings of stew and potatoes. Their mother was in a state of acute shock brought on by their announcement that they had found work at the palace; as a result, she was willing to cook whatever they asked for.

"Do you think there'll be any chocolates around?" Globula asked hopefully as they reached the top of the drive.

Conducta shrugged. "Dunno. We can have a snoop while we're doing dusting or whatever it was that book said."

The memory of the *Handbook* made Globula giggle. "'Rise at five to light the bedroom fires!' They should be so lucky!"

"We could set fire to the bedrooms," Conducta suggested. "We'd only be doing as we were told." She opened the door, and they walked in. The smell of roast chicken and apple pie still lingered heavily in the air, and the twins sniffed appreciatively. Following their noses along the corridors and down the kitchen steps, they arrived just in time to hear Bobby squealing in pain.

"Ow! Ow! Let go of my ears! That hurts — it really, really hurts! I promise I won't eat anything else! Please let me go! Please!"

Delighted, the twins gave each other a thumbs-up.

"Don't ever touch the food I cook." The voice was strange and yet familiar. Globula frowned. Where had she heard it before?

Conducta pinched her arm. "Grandma!" she hissed. "Isn't that Grandma's voice?"

Globula nodded. "But what's she doing here?"

"Let's see!" Her sister grabbed her, and they hurried inside — and froze, their eyes popping out of their heads and their mouths hanging open.

Mercy Grinder, who had been suspending Bobby by

his ears above a pan of boiling water, dropped him on the floor. "Twins," she said, looking the sisters up and down. "Housemaids." She pointed at a large fruitcake. "King Horace is waiting. Go to the dining room. Now!"

If Globula and Conducta had not been totally dazed by Mercy Grinder's appearance, they would have protested strongly at such a bald instruction. As it was, they meekly picked up the cake, and it wasn't until they were halfway up the stairs that Conducta regained enough presence of mind to whisper, "Was that Granpappy? Or did it just look exactly like him?"

"It wasn't his voice," Globula said doubtfully. "And I think it was a woman."

"Hmm." Conducta hated to be wrong about anything. "Do you think it might be Granpappy in disguise?"

"I suppose. . . ."

The twins climbed the rest of the stairs in thoughtful silence, but as they reached the top, Conducta exclaimed, "I've got it! We'll look at her hand! You remember it got burned? By Ma's brooch? We can see if there's still a scar. If there is, we'll know it really is Granpappy."

"Said you were sly. Knew I was right!"

Both twins jumped. They were passing a window, and Carrion was perched on the sill.

"Better be careful. Too sharp, and you'll cut yerselves."

Conducta and Globula turned to each other. "It must be Grandpappy!" they said together.

Carrion pulled at a tail feather. "It might be. Or it might not be. Word to the wise. Eyes and ears open . . . but mouths shut."

"But if it *is* Granpappy," Globula protested, "he'll look after us."

Carrion found this statement so incredibly funny he all but fell off his perch. Globula glared at him, and he managed to pull himself together sufficiently to gasp, "Look after you? Look after you? Old Malignancy's never looked after anything, ever. He'd have the breath out of yer body if he needed it. Or wanted it. Look at the way he's taken the voice from the old woman. Never asked, neither. Left her silent as a cabbage and about as much use." And he fanned himself with his wing in an effort to recover.

Conducta's eyes had sharpened. "So it *is* Granpappy," she said thoughtfully. "And he's stolen Grandma's voice."

Carrion stopped laughing. "Never told you that," he snapped. "Never. Never said any such thing." And with a couple of flaps of his wings, he was gone.

Globula jabbed her elbow in her sister's side. "Clever," she said admiringly.

"Yes." Conducta smirked.

Globula pushed at a nearby door. "Here's the dining room . . . oooh! Look! Is that the king?"

It was indeed King Horace, but a rather different King Horace from the man who had crossed the park earlier that morning. This King Horace had a bright red face, and his clothes were straining at the seams. There were smears of food down his bulging velvet front, and his chair was surrounded by crumbs; on the table in front of him were the remains of an apple pie and a sponge cake. Saturday Mousewater hovered in the background, clutching a well-licked bowl of chocolate mousse.

"Are you sure it's finished?" the king was asking. He sounded plaintive. "Isn't there even a little bit more? Just a teensy-weensy little spoonful?"

"'Tis all gone, Your Majesty," Saturday told him. "Truly." She caught sight of the twins and shivered before adding, "But there's a fruitcake just arrived, like."

King Horace beamed. "Fruitcake, eh? Now you come to mention it, I could fancy a slice or two. Bring it here, m'dears."

The twins advanced and placed the cake in front of

the king, who immediately cut himself an enormous chunk and stuffed it into his mouth.

Saturday took advantage of this activity to escape. "Princess Fedora said you were to report to her when you got here, then go to the kitchen," she said as she passed the twins. "She said she'd be in the upstairs sitting room, like. She's up there with Prince Tertius." She did not think it her place to add that the prince had been torn away from the food only by the strength of Fedora's personality. If he had had his way, he would have stayed with his father; on recovering from his cold and sticky lemonade shower, he had demanded cheese-and-pickle sandwiches and, with most uncharacteristic tenacity, had refused to move until Fedora agreed he could have his wish. Bobby had been sent for and had obliged by cutting the bread and cheese himself. The prince had then unwillingly followed his beloved, who, having taken charge of the sandwiches, refused to let him touch them until they were upstairs.

The twins shrugged. "S'pose we'd better go," Globula said. "Where's the upstairs sitting room, then?"

"At the top of the grand staircase," Saturday told them, then fled before she was asked to show them the way.

King Horace took no notice as the twins left the room. He was too busy finishing the fruitcake and peering around to see if there was anything else left to eat. "Might go and look in the kitchen," he decided. "Good woman, that Mershy . . . Mercy Grinder. Might ask for a little more of that chocolate mousse. Excellent stuff. Excellent! Or even a *lot* more. Yes! I'm king, aren't I? Can ask for whatever I want!"

Fortified by this decision, he set off to find his new cook. As he descended the stairs, he was alarmed to hear raucous shouting, but by the time he reached the bottom, there was only the sound of pans clattering and the delicious smell of fresh baking. Carrion, keeping a careful watch from the shadows, had had time to warn Mercy Grinder of the king's approach, and she had shut Bobby in a cupboard.

Bobby, whose only crime had been to make Tertius his cheese-and-pickle sandwiches, was both terrified and mystified. Crouched in the darkness, he wiped his nose with his sleeve. *She's weird,* he thought. *I'm going to ask Saturday about her. Saturday's OK, she is. If she wasn't here, I'd run away, and that's a fact.*

King Horace waddled happily into the kitchen. "Afternoon! Delighted to welcome you to the palace of Niven's Knowe. I'm the king, by the way. You can call me His Majesty. Or His Maj. We're all friends around here, dontcha know. How do you do!" And he held out his hand.

Mercy Grinder blinked. "Oh. What? Yes. How do," she said. Carrion cocked his head to one side. He had never heard either Mercy Grinder or, indeed, Old Malignancy sound surprised. But then again, such wholehearted enthusiasm in the presence of either character was an unknown. Hesitation, wariness, suspicion, sheer unadulterated terror — all of these were to be expected. A genuine smile and a welcoming handshake was a totally new experience.

The king went on beaming. "Excellent food. Really excellent. Don't know how you do it! Thought Mrs. Basket was good, but you — you're amazing! Don't suppose you could whip up some more of that chocolate mousse, could you? Never tasted anything like it!"

"Yes." Mercy Grinder blinked again.

"Splendid! Splendid! Get it sent upstairs, would you?" King Horace yawned. "Tush! Been tired all day. Bad dreams all last night, dontcha know. Dragons. Dreamed about dragons all night long — all Prince Marcus's fault, of course."

The pale eyes swiveled and fixed on the king. "Dragons?"

"Nothing to worry about, m'dear. Ancient history. Used to be a few roaming about the place, but they're long gone now. Don't you worry your pretty little head. Right! Must be off. Don't forget to send that mousse as soon as you can. Excellent! Excellent!" And the king took himself away.

It was fortunate he left when he did, as Carrion was unable to contain his mirth any longer. Shrieking with laughter, he flapped down from his perch behind the soup tureen and landed on the table. "'Pretty little head'!" he gasped. "'Pretty little head'! Strike me dead with a matchstick if that don't beat all!"

"Shut your beak, birdie, or I'll shut it for you!" It was Old Malignancy making the threat, and he was angry. Very angry.

His shout made Bobby jump, and he hit his elbow hard on the side of the cupboard. Carrion took no notice of the threat. He went on laughing.

Old Malignancy picked up a heavy meat cleaver and threw it, but the crow hopped neatly out of the way. "Get out of my sight!"

This time Carrion felt it best to obey; he gave one last derisive squawk and flew out the window.

Old Malignancy hissed, then opened the cupboard and pulled Bobby out by his hair. "What did you hear?"

Mercy Grinder was back—although there was still more than a hint of menace in her voice. Behind her, unseen, stood Saturday with her finger on her lips.

Bobby rubbed at his painful elbow. "Nothing," he whimpered. "Can't hear nothing in there. It's dark, and I don't like it. I won't cut no more bread, I promise."

He was given a sharp cuff around the ear, but Mercy seemed to believe him. She turned to go back to her cooking and saw Saturday. The cook scowled and made as if she was going to cuff the girl as well, but at the last moment she gave a sharp exclamation and pulled her hand back. "Trueheart!"

Saturday's eyes opened wide in astonishment. "No, ma'am. Saturday Mousewater, I be."

Mercy Grinder put her hand in the pocket of her apron. "Mousewater? A Mousewater in my kitchen?"

"Yes, ma'am." Saturday's knees were knocking, and the icy feeling in her stomach intensified. "If you please, I should be doing the dishes, like. . . ." She pointed at the enormous pile of pans and dishes that filled the sink to overflowing.

Before Mercy could answer, there was the clatter of feet on the stairs, and the twins came marching in. "We're to do as you say," they announced. Globula stuck out her tongue at Saturday. "Not as *you* say. Her!" And she jerked her thumb in the direction of Mercy Grinder.

"'S right." Conducta tweaked Bobby's nose. "They want the fire lit upstairs, so leave! Now!"

Mercy folded her huge hamlike arms, and her ice-pale eyes gleamed. "You go too," she told Saturday, and as Saturday scurried after Bobby, she turned to the twins. "Now, my little cankerettes, my sweetlings, my sour little plums, Carrion tells me you have seen through my disguise."

"It wasn't very difficult," Conducta began, but she stopped when she saw the scowl that appeared on her great-grandfather's face. "I mean . . ."

"Never mind." Old Malignancy pulled Fedora's advertisement out of his pocket. "You see this parchment . . . complete with royal seal?"

Globula didn't wait for him to finish. "There's *stacks* of that parchment in the dining room," she said. "We saw it there when we were being interviewed, didn't we, Conducta? It was on Lady High-and-Mighty's desk." She didn't explain that she had spent most of the interview trying to locate a box of chocolates or, indeed, anything else that might take her fancy.

Conducta sniggered. "It was there with her dear little gold pen." She pulled the pen out of her pocket and gave it a loving pat.

Old Malignancy rumbled approval. "Fetch me a sheet or two of that parchment. Run!"

"What if the king sees her?" Globula asked.

"The king will see nothing." Old Malignancy was in no doubt, and Conducta ran.

Two minutes later she was back, brandishing several sheets of parchment complete with the royal seal of Niven's Knowe. "He's asleep," she reported. "What did you put in that fruitcake? I pulled his beard, and he never even twitched."

"Lethargy," Old Malignancy told her. "Apathy. Eventually Total Oblivion . . . but first I have need of that foolish king's signature."

"Oooh!" Conducta sniggered. "Do you want his autograph?"

Old Malignancy glared at her, and she subsided. "Write!" He placed a piece of parchment on the kitchen table and began to dictate. Conducta, her eyes screwed up in concentration and Fedora's gold pen clenched in her hand, did her best to keep up.

"Stupid." Globula was hanging over her. "You don't spell *permission* like that. It's got an *r* in it."

"Such small niceties are of no matter," Old Malignancy announced. "Continue!"

As Conducta went on writing, Globula's eyes

opened wider and wider. "You're going to get them to let zombies back into the Five Kingdoms? And Deep Witches?"

"Nobody will be excluded. Now, I think we are done." The twins' great-grandfather picked up the parchment and studied it. "Yes . . . that will do. That will do well."

Conducta and Globula smirked. "So do we get a treat?" Globula asked.

"No." Old Malignancy had the air of someone about to make a joke, a joke that only he would enjoy. "I want you, my little cankerettes, to employ yourselves another way. Mercy Grinder has returned. Wash the dishes."

The twins, outraged, opened their mouths to complain, but they were unable to make a sound. Mercy went back to her chocolate mousse. Conducta slowly picked up a sponge and Globula a tea towel.

"Work, my little cankerettes. Work . . . First work, and then you shall have your reward. I have a task you will enjoy. Make sure the Mousewater leaves the palace. This is no place for her. No place at all, so see she goes. Do it in whichever way it pleases you."

The words were hardly more than a breath, but the sisters jumped as if they had been stung. Seconds later they were working as they'd never worked in their lives, calculating smiles on both their faces.

Chapter Eighteen

Gubble was making slow but steady progress. He had been briefly halted by a stone wall enclosing a vegetable garden, but after taking several short runs at it, he had reduced it to a satisfactory pile of rubble and walked over it. The owner—a small, skinny woman—had come storming out of her cottage followed by her eleven children; once she had actually set eyes on Gubble, she gathered them up like a mother hen protecting her chicks and beat a hasty retreat.

Only the oldest boy was left outside. "Oi! That's my mum's wall!" he yelled, but he got no answer as Gubble continued on his way.

The troll stomped heavily through the potato patch, straight through the rickety fence that marked the far side of the garden, and off into the field beyond.

"We'll see about this!" the boy said to himself. "The kids'll be running out and getting lost, and who knows what'll come running in through that gap." And with a determined look in his eye, he set off after Gubble.

Gubble continued on his way. By the late afternoon, the boy was not alone; another dozen offended property owners were trailing the troll. None of them was brave enough to confront him face-to-face, but there was an increasing sense of solidarity. Their estimates of the damage he had caused were also increasing as each mile passed; an impartial observer would have been astonished to hear that Gubble had not only knocked down a stone wall and a rickety fence but had also destroyed a barn full of best-quality hay, two cottages, a cow barn, and several brand-new pigpens.

"Shouldn't be allowed," they told one another. "He must belong to someone, though. If we follow him, we can claim!" The boy kept to himself; every so often he walked close beside Gubble and shouted in his ear, but the troll took no more notice than if he had been a buzzing fly.

With the coming of evening and the onset of a chilly wind, the number of followers began to drop; one by one, they fell away, muttering darkly as they did so. By midnight only the determined boy was left. As Gubble

rolled into a ditch in order to take a much-needed rest, the boy marched up to him. "You!" He bent over and stuck his finger into Gubble's chest. "You broke down my mum's wall. You've got to come back and mend it!"

Gubble was already asleep, but he began to dream he was being tickled. He chuckled before turning on his side and beginning to snore.

The boy tried pulling Gubble's nose, but a smile crossed the flat green face and the snoring grew louder. "DUH!" The boy stamped his foot in frustration. "Trolls! Well, you needn't think you're going to escape. I'm going to wait right here, and wherever you go, I'm going to follow you, so there!" And he found himself a clump of reasonably dry grass, curled himself up like a puppy, and did his best to ignore the steady droning noise coming from the ditch.

Gracie and Marcus had also been overtaken by the coming of darkness. Glee had shown signs of weariness, and Marcus had reluctantly agreed it would be best if they stopped for the night at Gorebreath Palace. Marlon and Alf, always happiest when the stars were out, had already taken themselves off, Marlon to report to the Ancient Crones, and Alf to tell the professor the events of the day. Great-Uncle Alvin was still peacefully asleep.

"We'll borrow Arry's pony," Marcus told Gracie as they led Glee into the Gorebreath Palace stable yard. "Then we can get to Niven's Knowe really early. If we leave at four in the morning, there'll be nobody to see us, so we can gallop nonstop!"

Gracie leaned against Glee's warm and comforting flank. "I think you might be right. What time does the sun come up?"

"Not sure." Marcus took Glee's saddle off and began to rub him down with a wisp of straw. "Tell you what . . . why don't we sleep here in the stable? If we get anywhere near Mother and Father, we'll end up having to have a formal dinner and they'll ask all kinds of boring questions. If we stay here, we can get up as soon as it's light. Glee should have had enough rest by then, and we can take Hinny as well — that's Arry's pony — and we'll get to Niven's Knowe before anyone's up and about."

"Shouldn't you ask Arry first?" Gracie wanted to know.

Marcus shook his head. "He won't mind. He's trying really hard to impress Nina-Rose, and he's hopeless at riding. He falls off all the time."

Gracie grinned, and the grin turned into a yawn. "Ooof. I'm tired. Shall I get Glee some oats?"

Between them they settled the pony down for the night. Marcus found a couple of old horse blankets, and Glee whickered softly as he realized he was to have company. Gracie was about to take her blanket into a corner when she remembered Great-Uncle Alvin. She opened Marcus's saddlebag, and a pair of sharp black eyes peered up at her.

"How are you feeling?" Gracie asked.

"I'll live." Alvin crawled out, spread his wings, and flew up to a roof beam. "Heard you talking." He sniffed. "Didn't think to ask my opinion, of course."

"I thought you were still asleep," Gracie said apologetically.

Alvin sniffed again. "Well, I wasn't. And I don't suppose for a moment you'll be interested, seeing as you know all the answers already, but I could—if I wanted to, of course—tell you where the dragons were stabled."

There was a respectful silence.

Great-Uncle Alvin enjoyed every second; he closed his eyes and reveled in the experience.

At last Marcus exclaimed, "WOW!"

"You're amazing, Great-Uncle Alvin," Gracie agreed. "And do you think that's where the egg might be?"

Alvin opened his eyes. "How should I know?

Lumiere hid the egg, didn't she, and it must have been well hidden or it would have been found long ago."

"Of course." Gracie hoped she sounded suitably chastened. "But you're quite right. The stable's the best place to start looking."

The elderly bat nodded. "So we'll set off at dawn tomorrow. Don't be late." And he turned himself upside down and closed his eyes.

Marcus grinned at Gracie as he spread out his blanket on the other side of the stable. "Don't be late!" he mouthed, and she did her best not to giggle.

"I heard that. I'm a bat." But Great-Uncle Alvin sounded fond rather than irritable.

Gracie smiled as she tucked herself deep into the hay. "Night-night, Marcus," she said sleepily.

"Night, Gracie," Marcus answered, then wondered if he should say anything else. After a moment's thought he added, "Sweet dreams"—and was immediately wide awake and covered in confusion. *What an idiot!* he thought. *What if she thinks I mean she ought to dream about me?* He waited, listening for an answer, but there was nothing but the sound of peaceful breathing. Obscurely disappointed, Marcus wrapped himself in his blanket and shut his eyes.

✳   ✳   ✳

In the palace of Niven's Knowe, only Carrion and Old Malignancy were awake. The twins were tucked up in a small attic bedroom, tired out by their first day of work. They had finished washing the piles of pots and pans and then, with infinitely more enthusiasm, proceeded to make Saturday's life a misery in every way they could. They had upset coal scuttles, knocked over wastepaper baskets, and spilled buckets of soapy water until she was worn out with cleaning up the mess. Now Saturday and Bobby were asleep in their respective rooms, and the three members of the royal family were also, as Saturday would have put it, down for the count. King Horace was snoring in his study, an empty chocolate-mousse bowl clasped in his arms. Princess Fedora was asleep in her beribboned and lace-looped four-poster bed, her *Handbook of Palace Management* tucked under her pillow. Prince Tertius, who had sneaked back to the dining room as soon as he could escape Fedora's watchful eye, was comatose under the table with his head on a large tin of cookies. His eyes had become unbearably heavy after he had eaten most of the substantial fish pie that Mercy Grinder had sent up for supper, and he had been unable to move any farther. Fedora had refused to look at the pie and had insisted on having a boiled egg sent up to her private boudoir.

The cook had tried to tempt her with more chocolate cake, but the princess had held her *Handbook* tightly to her chest like a talisman, and Bobby had returned to the kitchen with the cake untouched. This had not gone down well; Mercy had glowered angrily, and Bobby had sidled away as soon as he could.

Now Old Malignancy, his huge white bulk looming pale in the darkness, was moving slowly around the outside of the palace. Carrion was flying above him, giving a running report on what he could see through the windows. "The king's snoring his head off. . . . So's the prince. . . . Can't be comfortable, though. Must be strong stuff in that fish pie to put him out like that! What have we got in the attic? Let's have a peek . . . well, well, well. Those twins of yours ain't a pretty sight. Look just as nasty when they're asleep as when they've got their peepers open. . . . Already got a nice little stash of stuff they've filched from Her Majesty. . . . Oho! There's a thing to make your teeth curl! Bobby's got that Saturday's hankie in his fist. Can't see Saturday. . . . She's got her head under her pillow. Been crying, I'd say. . . . Let's go down a bit. Here we go. . . . Classy velvet curtains . . . and the princess is snoozing in among her frillies . . . but she's looking as if she's in a right ol' mood."

Old Malignancy made an impatient gesture as if he was brushing away something irritating. "The king and the prince are full of my food, and tomorrow will be wanting more . . . much, much more . . . and when I make my small and most reasonable request, they will be only too willing to agree. A change in the law will mean nothing to them now, nothing at all. But I see a problem."

Carrion flew down and perched on a statue. "A problem? Nah! What problem?"

Old Malignancy shrugged, and his enormous body rippled from head to foot. "To alter the laws of the Five Kingdoms, three royal signatures are needed— three at the least. King Horace's will be one. Prince Tertius's two. But Princess Fedora is different. Very different. She has a will of steel. How can I break her, Carrion? And that weak and watery prince does all she tells him."

After giving the back of his neck a good scratch, the crow suggested, "Chocolates. Not cake. Chocolates. What you might call the classy sort. And not a lot. Just a few. All elegant, like. A present from the prince to his lady. You'll have to make 'em strong stuff, mind."

"Chocolates . . ." Old Malignancy considered the suggestion. "Carrion, you have a dark and devious mind."

Carrion gave a delighted squawk. "That's me, boss. Now, if you're done for the night, I needs my shut-eye. Nice collection of trees down there in the park. Suit me nicely. Give me a chance to see if anyone's sneaking in the back way, too."

"Go." Old Malignancy was already deep in thought as he waved the crow away. "A hazelnut enrobed in a thick dark casing of richest chocolate, perhaps . . . or a delicate cream imbued with the scent of fresh pink roses . . . or maybe subtle violets . . ." And he moved smoothly back to the kitchen, making no sound.

In the House of the Ancient Crones, the night was very long. In room seventeen the Ancient One was crouched over the web of power, and the Oldest sat beside her. They did not speak; it was taking all their concentration and skill to keep the silver threads from knotting and twisting and breaking.

When Marlon flew into the kitchen in the early hours of the morning, the Youngest gave him a warning glance. "Don't bother them. There's trouble; I didn't go home last night. Looks like some kind of terrible evil has sneaked in through the borders, but we can't tell what or where. Edna and Elsie are only just managing to keep the web flowing. What's your news?"

Marlon gave a brief account of Great-Uncle Alvin's revelations and Gracie and Marcus's plans.

Val sighed. "Doesn't sound good to me."

Ever the optimist, Marlon waved a cheery wing. "The kid's a Trueheart."

Val gave him a disapproving look. "So she is. But she's also looking for something every evil thing is going to want, and the web's telling us some horrible character or other's already inside the kingdoms. Let's just hope Gracie's not heading into danger."

Marlon waved the other wing. "Danger-schmanger. She's got her uncle Marlon to keep an eye on her. No worries! All the same . . ." He hesitated.

"Yes?" Val prompted.

"Gotta go. Marlon Batster, ever the open eye. *Ciao!*" And he was gone.

Chapter Nineteen

The dawn light was still thin and gray when Great-Uncle Alvin took it upon himself to wake Marcus and Gracie. He woke Gracie first, and she sat up as he fluttered across to Marcus, who came to with a start and was on his feet almost before his eyes were open.

"I'll saddle Glee," he said. "You go and meet Hinny. You'll get on ever so well with her—she's just like a rocking horse. Arry used to fall off all the time, but now he hardly ever does. She's in the loose box next door. Oh, and have a look in the cupboard on the wall. There'll be apples and carrots in there—but don't give them all to Hinny. I'm starving, and I bet you are too!"

Gracie, who was so hungry her stomach kept rumbling, treated him to one of her sunniest smiles and went to look. There were indeed apples and carrots, and after making Hinny's acquaintance, Gracie helped herself. She took a handful back to Marcus and Glee, and the three of them munched companionably while Marcus finished saddling the pony.

"That's better," Marcus said as he gave Glee his apple cores. "I'll get Hinny ready, and we'll be off."

Ten minutes later, they were riding the ponies out of the stable yard and into the early morning, guiding them away from the cobbles and onto the soft grassy verge, where their hooves would make no sound. A mist hung over the fields, and Gracie became very aware of the silence. Even the birds were still asleep; when Hinny tossed her head and whinnied, it made Gracie jump. "Oh!" she said, and then, "Marcus! Have you seen Great-Uncle Alvin since he woke you up?"

Marcus shook his head. "I thought he was with you."

Gracie put her hand to her mouth. "Oh, *no*! How could we? We've forgotten him—"

"Nice to know you're thinking of me at last," said a sarcastic voice. The bat emerged, ruffled, from the saddlebag and landed on Gracie's shoulder.

"I'm so sorry," Gracie said in heartfelt tones. "I think it's because it's so early."

"Hmph," Alvin said. But he stayed on Gracie's shoulder, and as they turned out of the palace gates and set off toward the road to Niven's Knowe, he was still there. A moment later Glee broke into a canter, and Hinny followed suit; Gracie took a sharp breath, but she soon began to enjoy herself. They covered the miles steadily without pushing the ponies too hard, and it was still early when they reached Niven's Knowe.

Marcus pulled Glee to a walk and gave Gracie an inquiring look. "Shall we head straight for the palace? It's not far from here. If we ride across the grounds instead of going up the drive, we should be able to get reasonably near without being seen."

Gracie nodded. "Let's hope everyone's still asleep."

Great-Uncle Alvin gave a small gusty sigh. "If I was the smart young bat I once was, I'd fly over and check for you. Where's Marlon when you need him? Or young Alf? Nowhere to be seen. Typical. Only the aged still on duty—"

"Complaining again, Unc? Alf Batster, present and correct!" The small bat wheeled around their heads, making sure he was well out of his great-uncle's reach. "Want the palace checked? I'm your bat! Safety report coming up ASAP!" He waved cheerily and zoomed off in the direction of the palace—only to reappear a moment later. "Forgot to say. Prof sends his best wishes 'n' says you're to be careful. Says if you find the Thing We're Looking For"—Alf attempted to wink, shut both eyes by mistake, and saved himself from a crash landing by a whisker—"you're to take it to the House of the Ancient Crones. He'll meet you there. See ya!" And he was off again.

"Let's go!" Marcus picked up Glee's reins and led the way into the parkland that surrounded the palace.

The trees were widely spaced, and it was possible to keep the ponies at a steady trot as they threaded their way in and out of towering beeches and oaks and lofty pines. Gracie kept glancing around as they rode; she had a strong sense of something unpleasant close by, but she could see nothing but the trees and ornamental shrubs and bushes.

"The back door of the palace and the outbuildings are just over there." Marcus pulled Glee to a halt under a gnarled old oak tree. "Why don't we leave the ponies here for the moment and go the rest of the way on foot?"

Gracie nodded, and they dismounted.

Marcus tied Glee and Hinny to a low branch, then took Gracie's hand. "Come on!" he said, his eyes bright with excitement. "Let's go find a dragon's egg!"

"Shh!" Gracie looked agonized. "Don't even say it!"

"Sorry," Marcus apologized. "But it's OK, Gracie. There's no one around—it's just trees!"

Great-Uncle Alvin shook his head. "There's a lot more to a tree than leaves. Bad mistake."

Gracie shivered, her skin prickling. "I think you're right. There's something listening. I'm sure there is. . . ."

Marcus dropped her hand and strode on ahead, his cheeks flaming. Gracie, a small uncomfortable feeling in the pit of her stomach, followed him. A moment later they were out in the open. In front of them was a low stone wall, to their right an arched gateway. The Niven's Knowe crest was carved on the supporting pillars, and Great-Uncle Alvin snorted. "Look at that! Used to be dragons holding a shield! And now look at them! All hacked about! Could be anything. Looks more like dogs with a cannonball. Pshaw!"

Gracie was watching Marcus. He was crouched behind the shelter of the wall, beckoning. When she ran to join him, he said tersely, "If we go through the archway, we'll be in the yard. Where were the dragons kept, Great-Uncle Alvin?"

"Away from the horses," the bat said. "Tall stone building. Big doors."

Marcus nodded. "Oh! I know! They use it for the old carriages. Right. I'll start looking in there. Gracie, why don't you go and check the other outbuildings?"

Gracie didn't agree or disagree. She merely looked

at him, and although there was no hint of reproach in her blue-eyed gaze, Marcus blushed to the roots of his hair.

"I'm a toad," he said. "I really am. I'm sorry—come on. We'll go together." He took Gracie's hand, and they ran toward the gateway, Great-Uncle Alvin clinging to Gracie's shoulder.

As they passed under the arch itself, Gracie staggered and almost fell. Uncle Alvin fluttered into the air, and Gracie put out a hand to steady herself.

"You OK?" Marcus asked. He glanced back at the arch. "That was in the picture in the prof's book! I recognize it! And there were dragons carved here as well . . . Are you sure you're all right?"

Gracie nodded. "I'm fine. I just felt a bit weird for a second," and they ran on.

From the top of the gnarled old oak tree, Carrion was watching them with interest. "A dragon's egg. Well, I never. Well, well, well, well, well. Old Malignancy'll be interested in that. Very interested, indeed!" He spread his wings and flew.

Old Malignancy had spent the night perfecting a tempting selection of chocolates for Fedora, and the results lay in a small red velvet heart-shaped box on the kitchen table. Beside it lay Conducta's work of the evening before: a declaration to the effect that restrictions on entry to the Five Kingdoms were to be lifted by Royal Decree, and, as from the date of signature, all would be welcome whatever their background or personal leanings toward blood, mutilation, and general evil.

As Carrion made his report, the huge shapeless body of his master quivered and grew larger, and the pale eyes gleamed. Alf, swinging on the ivy surrounding the open kitchen window, gulped.

"A dragon's egg . . ." Old Malignancy wound his long sinuous fingers around and around. "Carrion — do you know what a dragon's egg can do?"

"Hatch a dragon?" the crow suggested brightly.

Old Malignancy gave a hollow chuckle. "It can do more . . . far more, if it is close to hatching. It can double and redouble my powers. Evil will make its way back to the Five Kingdoms, Carrion, and I shall see that it reaches every man, every woman, and every child. All will be corrupted, and Misery, Hunger, and Vice will prevail. And this egg . . . this dragon's egg . . . that will be my prize. I will watch over it until it hatches, and the dragon will grow strong in my ways. I shall teach it the ways of Evil, and those ways are all it will ever know. We will stride the kingdoms together,

he and I . . . and no one will stop us. No one!" He gave
an echoing high-pitched cry of ecstatic anticipation,
and the crow made a quick hop backward. Outside the
window Alf shivered uncontrollably.

"*Ark.*" Carrion recovered himself. "Sounds like a
barrel of fun and games. D'you want me to keep an
eye on the kiddywinks out there?"

Old Malignancy blinked and came back to reality.
"Watch, but do not let them see you. Let them find the
egg, and then we will strike. In the meantime, fetch my
little cankerettes. Drag them from their beds. I have
need of them."

Carrion nodded and flew off to wake the twins.
This was not easy; neither had any intention of getting
up until they felt like it. They buried themselves under
the bedclothes and ignored the crow's exhortations to
rise and shine. Carrion was finally driven to remark
that there were two intruders on the palace grounds
hunting for a dragon's egg. "Yer granpappy needs you
to sneak and spy. Valuable, that egg is . . . special."

The twins sat up, alert but suspicious. "What's in it
for us?" Conducta wanted to know.

"Word to the wise. Keep yer granpappy happy."
Carrion let out a raucous caw of laughter. "That's good,
ain't it? Happy Granpappy! 'Cause let me tell you,

ladies — one thing I do know, and I knows it well. If he ain't happy, he'll make sure nobody else is neither."

The twins had seen enough of their great-grandfather to believe this to be true. They looked at each other, then Globula said, "OK. We'll get up."

"Good thinking." Carrion gave her a leering wink. "Now, open this window. I need to check on the young adventurers down below."

Alf, now hovering in the shadow of the eaves, had only just time to swoop away before the crow flapped into the early morning sunlight. His heart beating hard in his small furry chest, he headed down to find Gracie and Marcus. "Boy!" he muttered as he flew. "Boy! Have I got news! Boy! Have I got *big* news! Boy—"

He didn't see Carrion coming. The first thing he knew there was a swirl of air followed by a massive blow that sent him spinning into blackness. Blackness punctuated by tiny stars and, in some dim outer world, a rasping voice. "Out of my way, bat! Gotta job to do. . . ."

Chapter Twenty

Gubble had also gotten up early, and the determined boy got up with him. The troll was not much improved by his night in the ditch; waterweed was draped around his neck, and his face was covered in mud.

"You could do with a wash," the boy said. He was taken aback when Gubble grunted and splashed water over himself, and even more surprised when the troll stomped into a neighboring field, pulled up two turnips, and offered him one. When the boy shook his head, Gubble grunted again and ate both. Moments later he set off, his eyes firmly fixed on the distant horizon.

"Oi!" The boy recovered his wits and hurried after him. "You're going the wrong way! You've got to come back and sort out my mum's wall!"

This time Gubble ignored him. He crossed the field and stomped through an apple orchard. The boy helped himself to a couple of apples and went after Gubble. As the sun rose higher, they tramped on and on, across village greens, into and out of a churchyard. On and on, through pig farms, hay fields, potato crops, and meadows where sheep were peacefully grazing. Farmers and shepherds shouted and waved their fists; Gubble took no notice. Seeing the boy walking purposefully behind the troll, several local characters with nothing better to do followed suit, urged on by a burly man carrying a pitchfork. "These trolls shouldn't be allowed," he announced to murmurs of agreement. "Cause damage wherever they go, they does! Should have been banned along wi' the zombies and the like."

It wasn't until they had left Gorebreath far behind and had crossed into the kingdom of Niven's Knowe that there was the sound of carriage wheels, and Gubble slowed a little. They were near enough to the road to see that it was Queen Bluebell's open carriage.

The queen, sitting high behind the coachman, raised her lorgnette to her eyes and inspected the ragged procession. "STOP!" she ordered. "What's all this? Revolution? Goodness me! It's Gracie Gillypot's troll! What are you doing here?"

Gubble, who was capable of ignoring even the Ancient Crones when it suited him, heard the word *Gracie* and came to a sudden and abrupt halt. "Niven's Knowe," he said. "Gubble go to Niven's Knowe. Palace."

"Goin' there myself," Bluebell announced. She indicated a nervous-looking woman sitting at the back of the carriage. "Found them a cook. Don't know if she'll do, but better than nothing. Hop in—I'll give you a lift."

Gubble walked around the carriage while he considered this offer. As he got closer, the woman looked increasingly anxious, and as he approached the door, she pulled her bag onto her lap and screamed. Gubble, taken by surprise, stepped backward, caught his foot on a stone, and sat down with a startled grunt. His head, never entirely secure, fell off, and the woman screamed again before gathering up her belongings and jumping over the side of the carriage. "You can stuff your job!" she shrieked. "Keeping company with trolls? I'd rather work with pigs!" And she fled away across the fields.

Queen Bluebell watched her go with an expression of martyred resignation. "Had a bad feeling about that one," she remarked. "Good cook but no stamina. No stamina at all." She turned to see whether Gubble had made up his mind and saw that the rabble had taken advantage of his headless state and was surrounding him. The man with the pitchfork was waving it threateningly;

only a lack of decision about whether he should skewer Gubble's head or his body was holding him back. Bluebell rose to her feet in fury—but before she could say a word, the boy had pushed his way forward and picked up Gubble's head.

"Here you are," he said, and thunked it onto the troll's shoulders.

"What did you do that for?" the pitchfork man asked angrily. "We could have done him in! Paid him back for what he did!"

The boy folded his arms. "It's not fair to attack him when he hasn't got his head on."

"Quite right, my lad," Queen Bluebell said approvingly. "Like your attitude! What's he done?"

"Ug." Gubble gave his head a reassuring pat. "Broke down wall. Gubble in a hurry."

"And that's not all, Your Majesty!" The burly man pushed forward.

Bluebell gave him an exceptionally frosty stare. "I don't remember asking for your opinion," she remarked in her most authoritative tone. "Am I to understand that you have a grievance against this troll?"

The burly man waved his pitchfork. "I surely do! Walked across my fields, he did—never asked nor nothing. Scared my cows witless!"

"Is that so?" Bluebell's eyebrows shot up. "And have you asked permission of King Horace to stand right here? I believe this particular field belongs to his estate."

The pitchfork was lowered while the burly man scratched his chin. "Well . . ." he began. "I can't say as I have, exactly. Didn't think about it."

"And I don't suppose Gubble thought about it, either." The queen folded her arms. "Now, run away home, and don't be a nuisance. If any of you has a genuine claim for damages, you can send it to me at Wadingburn Palace, but you'd better make sure it's a good one. I'll have no truck with time-wasters!"

The villagers melted away like snow in sunlight, leaving only the boy remaining.

Bluebell sat down in her carriage and inspected him. "Determined young fellow, aren't you?"

The boy nodded. "Our wall got broken down, and it needs putting back the way it was, or Amber and Heidi and Ben will be up to all sorts of mischief." He pointed at Gubble. "He did it."

"Fair enough. You're a sensible, plain-speaking boy," Bluebell told him. "We'll get your wall sorted out as soon as we can. I'd suggest I send a builder, though. Gubble has a facility for knocking things down, but I don't think his skills include building them back up again."

"Thanks, Your Majesty." The boy gave a brief nod. "I'll be getting home now that that's settled." He turned, then swung around again. "None of my business, but were you looking for a cook?"

"I certainly am." Bluebell leaned forward in her seat.

For the first time, the boy smiled. "I love cooking. Especially cake. My mum was a cook before she had all of us, and she taught me loads."

"In that case," Bluebell announced, "you've got a job. What's your name?"

"Marshling," the boy said. "Marshling Stonecrop."

"Hop into the carriage, Marshling, and I'll take you to meet your new employers. You can cook them breakfast. Gubble, are you coming with us?"

But Gubble had gone. Bored with waiting, he had stomped on toward the palace, taking, as always, the most direct route. Bluebell was just in time to catch sight of his solid figure disappearing into a clump of trees.

"We'll see him when we get there," she said. "Coachman! Drive on!"

Chapter Twenty-one

Old Malignancy was growing in both confidence and
size as each minute ticked by. The day had begun
well; Princess Fedora had rung her bell early, and
Bobby had come hurrying down to the kitchen to say
that she wanted a breakfast tray in her bedroom.

"'Boiled egg 'n' toast and a cup of tea' is what she
says, Mrs. Grinder," he rattled off. Fedora had said
a great deal more about the inadequacies of Prince
Tertius and the dangers of gluttony and greed, but
Bobby had no intention of passing this information
on. The princess was not, in his opinion, her usual
self; despite her ranting, she was curiously lethargic
and seemed unwilling to leave her bed. Her *Handbook
of Palace Management* was looking decidedly well
thumbed; Bobby noticed it was open at a page headed
"Unsatisfactory Servants: Constructive Criticism and

Ultimate Dismissal." A faint hope stirred in Bobby's mind; he whistled as he made his way to the kitchen.

"Egg and toast." Mercy Grinder nodded and clicked her fingers at the twins. "Lay a tray!"

The twins sullenly obeyed; they were not used to being up so early, and they suspected Carrion, now perched openly in a corner of the kitchen, of having tricked them. It was only when the red velvet box of chocolates was placed on the tray that they brightened.

Seeing their greedy looks, their great-grandfather abandoned his persona of Mercy Grinder and wagged a finger at them. "Not for you, my little cankerettes!"

As Saturday had been instructed to sweep and dust and polish the main rooms of the palace, Bobby was entrusted with taking the tray upstairs.

"We can do it!" Globula said eagerly—but the finger was wagged once more.

"The princess isn't used to you, my dears. Remember, Bobby. The prince sends his love with his gift of chocolates."

Globula, pouting, had had to be content with accompanying the page as far as Fedora's bedroom in order to hold open the door. A scuffle had taken place as Globula made one last attempt to acquire the chocolates, but when the tray was placed on Fedora's lap, the little heart-shaped box was still there.

"It's from the prince," Bobby explained when Fedora picked it up, and the princess smiled.

"Darling Terty! Maybe I'll forgive him after all."

Bobby had collected the dirty dishes from outside her door some half an hour later and taken them down to the kitchen. Seeing him come in, Old Malignancy had seized the box. Finding it empty, he had given an eerie shriek of triumph and held it high. "Gone!" he chortled. "Gone." When he saw Bobby staring at him in astonishment, his expression darkened. "Get to work!" And as Bobby scuttled out of the kitchen, Old Malignancy threw off his apron and swung around to the twins. "The Mousewater. She must go! My time is coming, and nothing must stand in my way!"

The twins sniggered and got up from the table. "Will we get chocolate if we get rid of her?" Conducta asked.

"You will get what you deserve." Old Malignancy's eyes were pebble hard, and Conducta shrank back.

"Come on, Sis," she said, and she and Globula flounced out.

Their great-grandfather spread his arms wide. "Soon, Carrion, soon the princess will be hurrying downstairs. She will be hungry, hungry for Mercy Grinder's food, and I will make my request. Three little signatures, Carrion . . . three little signatures, and the Five Kingdoms will be mine! Go and wait in the dining room. The prince is there; the king will join him, then Princess Fedora. Tell me the moment all three are ready for me!"

King Horace opened his eyes and found himself staring into an empty bowl. For a moment he couldn't think where he was or what he was doing, but gradually thoughts began seeping into his foggy brain. The first was: *chocolate mousse.* The second was: *It's morning and that's when I have breakfast.* And the third was: *I'm hungry.* He heaved himself out of his chair and went to ring the bell, but decided it would be quicker to give his order himself.

He was puzzled to find how difficult it was to squeeze himself through his study door; a vague idea that the palace had shrunk during the night crossed his mind. This idea was reinforced when he tried to make his way to the kitchen. "Shockingly narrow," he complained as he negotiated his way along the corridors. "Must have a word with . . . with someone." The strange confusion in his head was beginning to worry him, and he stood still and leaned his head against a pillar to see if the coldness of the marble would assist his thinking.

"Are you all right, Your Maj?" Bobby was standing beside him. "You look a bit the worse for wear, if you don't mind my saying so."

"I *feel* a bit the worse for wear," the king said, "and I'm hungry. Be a good boy and fetch me my breakfast."

"Certainly will. Eggs 'n' bacon? Mushrooms? That sort of thing?" Bobby asked. "Shall I bring it to the dining room?"

The king heaved himself away from the pillar. "In the dining room. Yes. But I want chocolate mousse."

Bobby dithered, then went somewhat unwillingly to do as he was told. He met Saturday as she came staggering down the back staircase carrying a bucket of dirty water and a mop. "King's a bit odd," he said in a whisper. "Wants chocolate mousse for his brekkie, and I don't think he was in bed last night. And he's *ever* so fat!"

Saturday looked anxiously over her shoulder. "'Tis that cook, Mercy Grinder. 'Tis her food, if you can call it that. Have you seen Prince Tertius? He's swelled up like a balloon under the dining table, like. 'Tis terrible, Bobby, terrible! And I don't —"

Footsteps were heard approaching, and Saturday

froze. Bobby gave her a swift wink of encouragement before hurrying to pass on the king's request. He was hardly out of sight before Globula and Conducta came marching around the corner; on seeing Saturday, they elbowed each other in vicious glee. "It's little batty Saturday," Globula sneered.

"That's right," Conducta agreed. "Little batty Saturday who drops everything she carries!" And she kicked Saturday's ankle.

Saturday screamed and dropped the bucket; it fell on the marble floor, and dirty water splashed in all directions.

"Oooh! Look what you've done!" Globula pointed to the mess. "Better clean it up, or you'll be in trouble."

"BIG trouble. You might even get the sack!" Conducta snapped her fingers under Saturday's nose. "Maybe you should leave. Run away before things get *really* nasty."

"Because that's what's going to happen." Globula tilted her head to one side and smiled a mocking smile. "Much better for little batty Saturday to go NOW!"

Saturday reeled back, her hands over her ears. "Leave me alone! I never did nothing to you!"

Conducta gave Saturday's hair a vicious tweak. "You're a Mousewater!"

Globula came even closer. "A horrid, *horrid* Mousewater. Run away, Saturday Mousewater—run away!"

And she gave Saturday such a hard slap that the girl found herself half skidding, half falling along the corridor. With an effort she stayed on her feet and ran as fast as she could to the front door of the palace. Wrenching it open, she staggered out into the sunlight.

Chapter Twenty-two

Marcus and Gracie, slipping through the door of the old stables, found themselves in a tall, dusty building. It was full of outdated coaches and outmoded carriages and a pile of broken wheels that reached nearly to the ceiling. There were windows set high in the stone walls, but they were covered in cobwebs and the light was dim. As Gracie's eyes grew accustomed to the shadowy gloom, she found she could see iron mangers fixed below the windows and could make out the remains of the stalls where the dragons were kept.

"Look!" Marcus whispered as he pointed to a heap of soot swept into a dark corner. "Do you think that's left from when the dragons breathed fire?"

Great-Uncle Alvin gave a derisive snort. "They knew better than to breathe fire in their own home. That'll be from when the crowds broke in after the dragons had been driven away. Set fire to the place, they did. If it hadn't been stone, it would've burned to the ground."

Marcus, aware that the elderly bat was still regarding him with disapproval, did his best to look meek, but there was something he needed to know. "Could the egg have gotten burned in the fire?"

"Of course not. Dear me!" Alvin fanned himself with his wing. "What *do* they teach you at school these days? A dragon's egg can be dropped into an inferno, and it'll come to no harm. Enjoy it, more like. And before you ask, young man, I checked this stable from top to bottom once the fire was out, and I didn't see a single sign of any egg."

"Then why are we here?" Marcus wanted to know.

Gracie felt it was time to intervene. "We've got to start somewhere. Perhaps one of the stones was loose, and Lumiere hid the egg behind it. . . ."

"Or maybe there never was an egg at all."

Marcus sounded gloomy, and Gracie looked at him in surprise. "What's the matter?"

The prince rubbed his eyes. "I don't know. It seemed so easy before we got here. But look at it!" He gestured at a moldering pile of leather and the clutter of harnesses beyond. "There's just so much stuff, and it's all been dumped since the dragons left. And the floor's solid stone slabs." He stamped his foot to demonstrate his point. "I thought it might have been floorboards—"

"Marcus!" Gracie stood very still. "Did you hear that?"

"What?" Marcus asked, puzzled.

"It sounded hollow!"

Marcus went pale, then sank to his knees. Carefully, he felt around with his fingers while Gracie pushed away the layers of dust, old leaves, and grit. "I can feel an edge. If I can just get my fingers under it, I might be able to shift it . . . but it's really heavy."

"Don't get your hopes up," Great-Uncle Alvin warned, but neither Marcus nor Gracie was listening.

"Let me help." Gracie knelt beside Marcus, and between them they managed to heave a broken section of stone up from the floor.

The bat fluttered down to look. "Nothing," he said. "Knew there wouldn't be."

"Bother." Marcus was about to let the segment of stone drop when Gracie stopped him.

"Wait a minute," she said. "Oh—I do wish it wasn't so dark!"

"I've got some matches somewhere," Marcus told

her, and holding the slab up with one hand, he dug in his pockets with the other. "Here."

Gracie took the battered box and struck a match. The light flared, and for a moment it was clear that under the stone slab was a carefully scooped hole, a hole lined with moss so old that when Gracie gently touched it with her finger, it crumbled into black dust. "Can you see the shape?" she said breathlessly. "It's exactly the shape of an egg!"

"But the egg's gone," Great-Uncle Alvin said as the match went out. "So that's not a lot of use."

Gracie stood up as Marcus dropped the stone back into place. "But it *is* useful! The egg was here—I *know* it was. My fingers feel . . . I don't know how to describe it. Tingly. So someone must have moved it."

"Maybe the dragon boy took it away," Marcus wondered.

But Gracie took no notice. She was standing with her hands clasped together and her head on one side as if she was listening to a secret message. "Oh . . ." she whispered. "Of course! The archway . . ."

Great-Uncle Alvin and Marcus stared at her. She was quivering with excitement. "Don't you remember? I nearly fell over when we ran through. I felt that same tingling feeling then, only much much stronger.

It made me feel almost dizzy, it was so strong—but I didn't know what it meant—"

"Come on!" Marcus was already at the door. "Let's go!" He peered cautiously out into the yard. "Lucky they can't see us here from the palace. None of the windows faces this way, and the main drive's on the other side."

It took them only seconds to retrace their steps. As they drew close to the archway, Gracie felt tingles run through her entire body. "It's there," she whispered. "I'm sure it is."

Marcus was already pushing and shoving at the blocks of stone. "How could it be hidden here? Do you think one of these pulls out?"

Gracie didn't immediately answer. She was standing underneath the arch with her eyes shut. After a moment she said, "It's so odd. I know it's here somewhere, but I can't place it. The tingles seem to come from all around me."

"But we've got to find it." Marcus scrubbed at his hair in frustration. "Can you tell if it's on one side more than the other?"

Gracie opened her eyes again. "No. At least—" She stopped midsentence. "What's happening down there? Look! Near the tree where we tied the ponies. The bushes are shaking . . . Oh! It's GUBBLE!"

Gubble emerged, brushed the remains of a bird's nest off his head, and stomped steadily on.

Gracie waved encouragement, while Marcus picked up a stone and began to tap and chip at the arch.

The troll came puffing up to join them. "Not heavens no. Niven's Knowe," he remarked in the manner of someone finishing a conversation that had been going on for some time. "Gubble help prince." And he walked straight into the left-hand pillar—which wobbled, shook, then collapsed with a rumble and a loud crash.

The openmouthed Gracie and Marcus were left staring at the remains. Underneath the wreckage lay an egg—dull green, and in no way spectacular, but neither could take their eyes off it.

"Pick it up, Trueheart," Great-Uncle Alvin whispered. "Pick it up."

Gracie bent down and carefully lifted the egg from the rubble. It felt cold and was heavier than she had expected. She stroked it with her fingers as Marcus exclaimed, "We've found it! We've actually found it!"

"Yes," Gracie said. "Great-Uncle Alvin, can I ask you something?"

Alvin didn't answer. He was leaning forward and listening intently to something neither Gracie nor Marcus could hear. "Alf! He needs help!"

"Alf? Where?" Marcus could see no sign of the little bat. Gracie didn't look up. She was still staring at the egg in her arms.

"Quick!" Uncle Alvin flapped his wings furiously. "Quick! Come on, Trueheart! He's in trouble! In the yard!" He zigzagged away as fast as his ancient wings would allow, and Marcus hurried after him. Gracie, after tying her cloak tightly around her so the egg was held close to her heart, followed as fast as she could.

Gubble watched them go, then bent to inspect the rubble. "Egg," he murmured. "Egg sandwiches. Good Gubble. Gracie pleased." And he turned his attention to the other stone pillar.

They found Alf crawling across the cobbles, his wings dragging, and his fur matted. "Danger!" he gasped. "Terrible danger!" As Marcus and Gracie crouched down beside him, he waved a claw toward the palace. "There's a horrible bird and there's a hideous THING in the palace kitchen, and there's something *dreadful* going on, and do you know what, Miss Gracie?"

"Oh, Alf!" Gracie scooped him up. "What happened?"

Alf trembled in her hands. "In the kitchen . . . this huge white thing! With white eyes! It's evil, Miss Gracie, it really really is. And it knows about the dragon's egg, and it wants it because dragons' eggs make you more evil, and, Miss Gracie, it knows you're looking for it! That horrible bird was watching us under the trees!"

Marcus stood up. His face was as white as chalk, and he swallowed hard before he spoke. "That's my fault. It was me who said about the dragon's egg. I'm going to the palace right this minute. I'm going to find the thing in the kitchen and get rid of it, or at least try to stop it from getting any farther. Gracie, you take the egg and get away from here as fast as you can. And . . ." He swallowed again. "I'm sorry. I'm really, really sorry—"

"Hold the heroics, kid." Marlon swooped into view in a leisurely curve designed to conceal the excessive speed at which he had traveled since leaving the House of the Ancient Crones. "Uncle Marlon's back in the action. And here's a suggestion. Go for cunning. Deviousness. Walk straight in and you could walk into big trouble."

Gracie looked at him. "What do you mean?"

"Need to check what's going on," Marlon said. "The crones have spotted evil. Evil, big-time. Give me five, and I'll be right back. *No problemo!*"

Marcus watched as the bat zigzagged away. He was truly ashamed of himself, and he desperately wanted to show Gracie that he could put things right by launching himself into the thick of the danger, but he was also aware that this could be bravado rather than bravery. He hesitated, then said, "You know what, Gracie? I've absolutely *got* to go and see for myself. It'll be all right — when Terty and I were little, we were always playing spies. We used to watch the formal dinners and laugh our heads off. I promise I won't be seen."

Gracie gave him her most luminous smile. "You mean, *we* won't be seen. I'm coming with you."

"Don't know what Unc'll say." Alf, perched on an upturned flowerpot, was recovering fast. He smiled smugly as Gracie and Marcus ran toward the palace. "I knew she'd go with him. True love 'n' all that."

Great-Uncle Alvin snorted. "Love, nothing. What about that egg? She's putting it in danger! And that," he added rather more thoughtfully, "isn't at all like a Trueheart. Hmm . . ."

He and Alf looked at each other. No word was spoken, but seconds later they were flying after Marcus and Gracie.

When Marlon made his way back five minutes later, eager to report on the twins and Mercy Grinder, he found the yard deserted. Soaring up into the sky to get a better aerial view, he was rewarded with the sight of a headless Gubble sitting among the remains of the now totally demolished stone archway. "Leave 'em for five minutes and they lose their heads," Marlon remarked to himself. "Hang on! What's he got there?" And he increased his speed.

Gubble's head looked up from a patch of dandelions. "Help. Find Gracie. Find Gracie NOW!"

Marlon's attention was entirely concentrated on the grit-covered object clutched in Gubble's arms. "My goodness," he exclaimed. And then, pulling himself together, "Right! Follow me!"

"Can't," said the head.

Marlon shook out his wings, took a deep breath, and issued instructions at such speed that the troll became hopelessly muddled. His head, when finally back on his shoulders, faced the wrong way. Marlon, suffering from intense frustration, snapped, "No time to change it. You'll have to walk backward. Come on — this way!"

Chapter Twenty-three

As Queen Bluebell's carriage came to a halt outside
the main entrance to the palace of Niven's Knowe,
she was greeted by the sight of the weeping Saturday.
Weeping housemaids were a common phenomenon
and, in Bluebell's wide experience, easily dealt with. She
pulled a handkerchief from her bag with a practiced
flick of the wrist. "Now, now," she said briskly. "Blow
your nose, and then we'll have a nice cup of tea. Was
it the butler who upset you? Or are you in love with a
footman?"

Saturday took the hankie and blew her nose hard.
"Oh, Your Majesty—it's them twins, like. Oh—I
can't bear it anymore!"

Bluebell patted Saturday's shoulder. "Twins? What
twins, my dear? I don't remember King Horace
employing any twins."

If Saturday had not been so overwrought, she might have stayed silent, but the queen's sympathetic gesture was too much for her. "Oh, Your Majesty!" she wailed. "Everyone's gone! Mrs. Basket and Mr. Trout and the footmen and everybody! Only me and Bobby are left, like. And there's that Mercy Grinder in the kitchen, making everybody blow up like balloons . . ."

Saturday had lost the queen's attention. Bluebell had heard enough to make her realize there was a serious problem, and she had never been one to shirk her duty. "You stay here," she ordered, and with a shake of her skirts she sailed into the palace.

Marshling Stonecrop, who had been listening with interest, immediately leaped out of the carriage and grabbed Saturday's arm. "Blow up like balloons? This I have to see!"

"Oh, no!" Saturday gave a loud wail. "Don't make me go back in there! Please don't!"

"Well . . ." Marshling gave Saturday a hard stare. "Is it really that bad? Or are you just a scaredy-cat?"

"'Tis terrible! That Mercy Grinder—she be evil! And the twins, too!"

Marshling decided Saturday's terror was genuine. "Is there another way in?"

Saturday nodded. "The back door."

"Right," Marshling said. "Around the other side, I'd guess. See you later!" And he marched off at a determined trot.

Saturday wavered, then ran after him, terrified at the thought of being left alone.

As they turned the corner of the palace, Marshling came to an abrupt halt. Saturday looked around in surprise, stared, then screamed as she saw a solid green troll standing nose to nose with Bobby. Then, realizing that the troll's body and head were facing in opposite directions, she screamed again.

Marlon, hovering overhead, rolled his eyes at this demonstration of human foolishness. "Keep going, troll!" he squeaked, but Gubble, confused by the noise and the fact that he was obliged to walk backward, stayed where he was.

"'S all right, Saturday," Bobby said through chattering teeth. "He wants to get inside the palace. I won't let him hurt you."

"He won't hurt anybody." Marshling stepped forward and gave Gubble a pat on the back. "Hello, Gubble. Why is your head on back to front? And what are you carrying?"

Gubble indicated the palace with a jerk of his chin. "Find Gracie."

"He keeps saying that." Bobby shook his head in bewilderment. "But I don't know who he's talking about."

"Gracie." Gubble tried again. "Ug. Gubble find Gracie . . ." He forced his very small brain to make one last supreme effort. "Pillypot!"

Marshling whistled. "That Queen Bluebell said he was Gracie Gillypot's troll. And the queen's in the palace. Maybe Gracie is, too. Come on, Gubble." And he set off once more, arm in arm with Gubble. Marlon sighed with relief and zoomed after them.

"Wow!" Bobby sounded admiring. "That boy knows what he wants, doesn't he?"

Saturday nodded agreement. "He wants to see the king and the prince, like. I told him they was all swelled up . . . Oh, Bobby! Whatever shall we do?"

Bobby was still staring after Marshling. "I think we should go, too," he decided. "I've never seen a troll that close before. If it's a good one, do you think it might get rid of that horrible Mercy Grinder?"

"Oh!" Saturday clasped her hands together. "Oh! That would be wonderful! Come on!"

Even at first glance, Queen Bluebell could see things were not as they should be: the floors were unscrubbed, and a bucket was lying on its side in a pool of dirty water. With a loud "Hmph!" she headed toward the dining room. Striding through the doors, she was astonished to see her old friend King Horace up to his whiskers in chocolate mousse, while Prince Tertius was sitting under the table eating spaghetti Bolognese with a teaspoon. Both the king and the prince were enormously swollen; when they saw the queen, they grunted a welcome but went on eating.

Marcus, crouched low outside the window, looked around at Gracie and saw she was as alarmed as he was. Alf began to shake, and Great-Uncle Alvin twitched.

"Really!" Queen Bluebell the Twenty-eighth of Wadingburn drew herself up to her full height. "Whatever is going on here? And what's *that*?" Her eye had fallen on Carrion, who was observing her with an unwinking eye from the back of a chair. "Shoo! Shoo, you horrid thing!"

"The bird's all right." The king was talking with his mouth full. "Belongs to our cook. Mercy Grinder. Fabulous woman. Fabulous! Couldn't do without her."

"Quite right." Tertius's sleepy voice floated up from under the table. "She's a wonder. Don't know where she came from, but she's a wonder, ain't she, Daddy-o?

And all she wants is for us to write our names on a piece of paper so she can keep them safe forever and ever. She's a . . . a . . . haughtygraph hunter. Hunts haughtygraphs. Told us she's got hundreds and thousands of . . . of haughtygraphs. Just waiting for ours . . . ours and Feddy's. Darling Feddy. She'll be down for her brekkie soon. And when we've signed, we're going to have cherry tart and raspberry custard and ice cream and—"

"What piece of paper?" There was a steely note in Bluebell's voice, and Carrion slid from his perch. With a couple of wing beats, he was out of the dining room, and seconds later he was in the kitchen.

Old Malignancy looked up, his huge shapeless body quivering with suppressed excitement. "The princess? Is she there?"

"Nope." Carrion shook his head. "But another royal's arrived. Better get some tea and cookies up there, pronto. She ain't the chocolate-mousse type, and she's asking awkward questions."

Snatching the parchment off the table, Old Malignancy smoothed it with long, trembling fingers. "Fate is on my side, Carrion. It seems we can do without the troublesome princess. The third signatory has been delivered! Once the document is signed, I can step out as my own true self, and the laws of the Five Kingdoms will fall away." He gave a self-satisfied chuckle. "And the power of the web will be broken forever, broken because of my incomparable skills and superlative cunning—"

"You ain't there yet," Carrion said sharply. "And if you don't get that old bag sorted out pretty soon, I'd say she was the type to call out the army."

Old Malignancy gave him a cold look but went to the cupboard and took out a plate of sugar buns—just as the twins came tumbling in, grinning from ear to ear.

"She's gone, Granpappy! She's gone! Saturday Mousewater—we've got rid of her forever and ever and EVER!"

"Be silent." The words were quiet, but the twins lost their smiles and stood still as statues in the doorway. Their great-grandfather ignored them as he took the boiling kettle from the fire and arranged a teapot and cups on a tray. "Take this upstairs," he ordered, handing Conducta the plate of buns. "Make sure these are eaten. All of them, do you hear? Or you will be sorry. Very sorry, indeed." His eyes glittered. "Carrion, go with them." He opened his arms in a grandiloquent gesture. "Return and tell me when the time has come to claim my kingdom."

Globula picked up the tray; moments later she and

her sister appeared in the dining room. "We've brought tea and buns," Conducta announced as Globula thumped the teapot down on the table.

Queen Bluebell raised her lorgnette and peered through it, pursing her lips. "That is no way to serve tea! And do you not wear uniforms? Where are your aprons?"

Globula folded her arms and scowled, but Conducta, more cunning, handed the queen a sugar bun on a plate.

Bluebell took it but went on with her questioning. "Where do you come from? Where did you work before?" As she waited for the answer, she took a large bite. At once her eyes began to roll alarmingly, and she lurched into a chair.

Her horrified expression made Globula double up with laughter. "Yah! Old bag!" she jeered.

"Shh!" Conducta pulled at her arm. "She's got to eat more."

But she was too late. King Horace reached across the table, helped himself to the remaining buns, and demolished them in three mouthfuls.

"Oops!" Conducta and Globula looked at each other and nodded in unspoken agreement. Sliding past

Queen Bluebell, they sank down behind a large sofa at the far end of the dining room. "We can watch what happens from here," Globula whispered. "And guess what? I've got a treat for us!" She patted her pocket and licked her lips.

Carrion, who had observed everything, decided the moment had come to report to Old Malignancy — but he did not have to go far. The billowing figure was already outside the open door. So certain was he of success that he was ready and waiting, a pen and the parchment in his hand. He surged through the doorway; just one glance reassured him that there would be no opposition. King Horace was drooping over his bowl, and Tertius was dozing under the table.

Queen Bluebell hiccuped, then peered blearily around. "Who did that? Rudeness! Such rudeness!"

"Your Majesties," Old Malignancy said in a voice like an oiled knife, "may I trouble you for your autographs? A kindness for a poor cook, a kindness much appreciated."

King Horace nodded. Queen Bluebell smiled a lopsided and foolish smile. "Of course," she said. "Of course."

Prince Tertius held up his hand. "Whatever you say,

Mercy Grinder. Whatever you say. 'S long as we get our yummy, scrummy raspberry custard."

Carrion gave a raucous squawk of laughter. "Custard! *Ark!* Five Kingdoms signed away for a bowl of custard!"

On the other side of the window, Marcus gave a stifled gasp and jumped to his feet. Gracie, holding the egg very close, did the same. Together they tiptoed away as fast as they could go, the bats flying above them.

"I've got to stop them from signing that paper!" Marcus's voice was shaking. "The Five Kingdoms are in terrible danger—and I'm going to go in there. I don't care what that horrible thing does to me; she's got to be stopped. And you absolutely mustn't let her get her hands on that egg. Run away, Gracie. Take Hinny, and get away from here. Go to the crones."

Gracie took a deep breath. "Marcus . . . do you trust me?"

Marcus was surprised by the question. "Of course I do. Why?"

"Well . . ." Gracie hesitated, then said, "I think we should go in there together. There . . . there's something I must say to that creature. I have to."

"What?" Marcus stared at her, his mind whirling.

"What can you possibly say that's going to stop this? Gracie, we haven't got time to argue. I've got to go *now,* or I'll be too late—"

Gracie put her hand on his. "Please, Marcus. Just trust me."

Marcus went on staring at her. He was a prince of the Five Kingdoms; it was his right to defend them. Every bone in his body was aching to fight, to take action . . . but it was Gracie who was standing in front of him. Gracie, who was looking at him with her clear blue eyes and asking him to trust her. "OK," he said, and swallowed hard. "OK. Say what you have to. But we have to get there before they sign anything, so come on! RUN!"

And they ran.

Chapter Twenty-four

King Horace, Prince Tertius, and Queen Bluebell did not hear Carrion. They watched with glazed expressions as Old Malignancy, already smiling a triumphant smile, billowed his way across the floor. As he heaved his enormous body toward King Horace, the door leading to the royal apartments burst open, and a shrill voice exclaimed, "Terty! How *dare* you give me an empty box of chocolates! I thought you were sorry for being such a greedy horrible pig—and you weren't! You're mean, and I hate—" Fedora stopped as she took in the scene in front of her. "You're eating AGAIN? And why's Mercy Grinder here? What's going on?"

Old Malignancy turned, and the force of his cold stare made her catch her breath and stagger against the wall. "Leave us!" he hissed. "Little fool. Leave us!"

"Oh! I say!" Tertius, despite the numbing gray fog that filled his head, gave a muffled cry of protest. "That's my darling Feddy you're talking to!"

"*Dearest* Terty! You're so brave! Save me!" Fedora flew across the room and hurled herself under the table and into her beloved's arms.

Old Malignancy rolled forward, his grossly swollen body now half filling the room. "Sign," he ordered, and he handed King Horace the parchment and pen. "Sign!"

King Horace obediently took the pen and parchment and signed his name.

"Just a minute!" Gracie was standing in the doorway, Marcus close behind her.

Old Malignancy swayed around with an echoing roar of anger, but when he saw Gracie, he was suddenly silent. "A Trueheart," he hissed. "If I'm not much mistaken, it's a Trueheart. Well, Trueheart, you are fortunate. Very fortunate. You will see me restore the Five Kingdoms to their rightful state . . . a state of Evil. Enjoy, Trueheart. Enjoy!" He turned back to the table and pushed the parchment in front of Queen Bluebell. "Sign!"

As Queen Bluebell the Twenty-eighth of Wadingburn drowsily lifted her hand and did as she was told, Gracie took an urgent step nearer. She was finding it difficult to breathe, and her heart was racing in her chest; her mouth was dry with fear, but she forced herself to speak. "Wait! I've something to offer you. Leave the Five Kingdoms, and I'll give you this." She opened her cloak and held up the dragon's egg, desperately hoping her shaking hands would not let it slip. "A dragon's egg in return for the Five Kingdoms. What do you say?"

"Gracie!" Marcus was aghast. "Gracie! Stop it! You can't!" He reached for the egg, but Gracie moved away from him.

Old Malignancy studied the prince and grunted with satisfaction as he saw that the horror on Marcus's face was real and unfeigned. A fierce anticipatory fire blazed in his eyes, and he held out his hand. "Give me the egg."

"Not until you tear up that document." Gracie did not move.

There was a long silence, and then Fedora spoke from under the table. "You should do as she says, 'cause I'm never going to let my darling Terty-pops sign your horrid paper. So there!"

Old Malignancy said nothing, but the look he gave Fedora made her squeal and hide her face in Tertius's chest.

"Tear up the document," Gracie repeated.

Old Malignancy picked up the parchment and tore it in half, then again and again, and scattered the pieces on the floor.

"The egg is yours," Gracie told him, and with a little sigh, she placed it in Old Malignancy's outstretched hands.

At once he began to laugh—a hideous, mirthless sound that made icy shivers run up and down Marcus's spine. "A Trueheart? You are no Trueheart. You are only a fool! Do you not know that now that I have the egg in my hands, I have more power than you can ever oppose? I need no document now. The Five Kingdoms are mine to take—mine, mine, MINE!" And Old Malignancy raised his massive arm.

Marcus leaped forward with a yell, but Gracie stayed very still, and the blow, when it reached her, fell lightly on her shoulder.

And it was Old Malignancy who shrieked, shrieked so loudly that the chandeliers shattered into a thousand tiny fragments of glass, and the whole room glittered as if spread with fallen stars. "Tricked!" he screeched, and dropped the egg as he made another lunge forward, only to be held back by the folds of his own flesh as his monstrous body deflated and sank toward the floor. "Tricked!" A puzzled expression crossed his doughy face as he glowered at Gracie. "But a Trueheart cannot lie. . . ."

"It wasn't a lie," Gracie said sadly. "It *is* a dragon's egg. Truly. But it's dead. That egg will never, ever hatch."

Old Malignancy closed his eyes and began to breathe in short panting gasps. The hanging flesh and the sagging bags of skin quivered and shook, then began to shiver and shrink, and as Marcus and Gracie stared, it became horribly obvious that he was returning to his original shape.

All of a sudden, his eyes snapped open. "Don't think you're done with me yet," he hissed. "Face me out, Trueheart! Face me out! Evil against truth and goodness . . . who will win?" And he looked deep into Gracie's eyes.

Gracie looked straight back. She could feel the strength of his gaze; whirling dark thoughts spun into her mind, thoughts of unkindnesses, slights, cruelties . . . but she kept them at bay as best she could.

Old Malignancy took a step forward, and Alf twittered anxiously from a curtain rail. "You can do it, Miss Gracie," he squeaked. "You can do it!"

Gracie heard him, but Old Malignancy increased

the force of his stare, and she had no choice but to concentrate on him and him alone. Shadows floated around her, memories of her unhappy childhood, memories of a lonely cold cellar, of shouting, of harsh beatings . . .

"Don't give in, Trueheart!" But Great-Uncle Alvin had a tremor in his voice—and Old Malignancy heard it.

"See her falter," he whispered. "See her fail. . . ."

"But she won't!" Marcus stepped forward and stood firm at Gracie's side. "She's a Trueheart through and through. She'll never fail."

Gracie took a long deep breath. "That's right!" she said. "Never!" And she opened her eyes wide and gave Old Malignancy one of her most beaming smiles.

He blinked, the tension between them broke, and with an agonized cry of defeat, the figure sank into a sodden, shapeless mass. "Carrion!" he called, but there was no strength in his voice. "Carrion!"

The crow flapped down, clicked his beak as he inspected his master, then shook his head. "No honor among the wicked," he said cheerfully. "Had yer chance and lost it." And he retreated to his chair and began to preen his feathers.

"My little cankerettes! Where are you?"

The twins came out from behind the sofa, their faces smeared with chocolate.

"Help me! Help your dear old granpappy, my little dears," Old Malignancy begged. "Do what you do best, little cankerettes. . . . Whistle and spit for me. Whistle and spit. . . ."

Conducta and Globula stood and gazed at their great-grandfather, their faces completely unmoved. Then they looked at each other.

"Those chocolates you made," Conducta said accusingly. "They were *disgusting!*"

"*Revolting!*" Globula agreed. "Just like ashes!"

Old Malignancy began to tremble with the faint echo of a terrible anger. "Mousewater," he whispered. "There is Mousewater in you yet . . . and I cast you from me!"

"Oh, no, you don't." Globula folded her arms. "*We* cast *you* out! We're going home to Mother."

"That's right!" Conducta stamped her foot. "Maybe it's not so bad being a Mousewater. Well, at least a bit of a Mousewater. At least we'll never end up like YOU!" She leaned forward and stuck out her tongue. "Do you know what you are, old Granpappy Canker? You're a failure—and we don't like failures." The twins linked arms, and with a toss of their heads, they marched out of the dining room, slamming the door behind them so hard that the walls shook.

Old Malignancy moaned and dragged his sagging body across the floor. With one last heave, he hauled himself up, crashed through the window, and slithered into the sunshine. There was a low keening wail that flowed on and on and on; at long last, it grew faint and faded into silence.

Alf, still on his curtain rail, gave a startled squeak. "Worms! Miss Gracie—that thing's turned into worms!"

Alf was right. The gargantuan white body had vanished; the white clothes were strewn empty over the grass, and wriggling out from underneath were long white worms that twisted and squirmed before vanishing deep into the earth.

Chapter Twenty-five

Back in the dining room, there was a remarkable change in the atmosphere. King Horace yawned and rubbed his eyes. Queen Bluebell hiccuped, apologized, and sat up straight with the air of someone who has fallen asleep without meaning to and who is likely to challenge any accusation that her eyes ever closed. Fedora and Tertius stayed under the table; Tertius was kissing Fedora's nose, and she was giggling happily.

"Wheeee!" Alf zigzagged down to land on Gracie's shoulder. "You did it, Miss Gracie! You did it!"

"That's right. Well done." Marcus sounded strained. "Well done, Gracie." He paused, then said stiffly, "You could have told me the egg was addled."

Gracie sighed. "No, I couldn't. Dear Marcus—don't you see? If I had, you would never have tried to stop me, and that . . . that thing wouldn't have believed me. And then it would have won."

Marcus grunted. "I could have pretended to try and stop you. I'm not entirely useless, you know."

He was rewarded with a smile. "You're anything but useless! If you hadn't come to stand beside me, I'd never ever have been able to keep going. And you did it even though you were cross with me, and that made it all the better." Her cheeks were very pink as she went on, "And do you know what? That was the action of a real Trueheart."

Marcus shifted uncomfortably before looking back at Gracie. "Thanks," he said. "That means a lot to me. Thank you." There was another pause, and then he added, "But I can't help wishing we'd found a live dragon's egg."

"But you did, kiddo," said a squeaky voice, and Marlon swooped into the room. "You did. Apologies for the delay, but the troll doesn't travel fast. Navigational problems."

"Ug." Gubble came stomping backward through the door, his dusty burden still clasped to his chest. He handed it to Gracie, and as she took it from him, she could feel its warmth and the beat of a heart deep inside. "Egg," Gubble announced. "Egg for Gracie. Gubble good?"

Gracie nodded. "Very good, indeed. Very, *very* indescribably and wonderfully good."

"Wow!" Marcus was alight with joy.

"We'd better go," Gracie said. "We'll take it to the crones, and then back to its parents." She handed the egg to Marcus, who took it reverently as Gracie walked to where the other egg was lying discarded by the wall. She picked it up and cradled it in her arms. "And we'll give this one a proper burial. Poor, poor thing . . . OH!"

"What is it?" Marcus stared at her.

"I think it's alive! I felt it move! And LOOK! It's started to glow! Whatever's happened to it?"

It was Carrion who answered. "Trueheart effect," he said. "You must be a good 'un, too. Trueheart through 'n' through, the way you carry on. And did nobody ever tell you? Dragon's eggs double yer power." He peered sourly at Gracie. "Gets into the air, as well. Like swapping winter for summer. Any minute now, I'll be singing 'Twinkle, Twinkle, Little Star.' Not my style, so I'll be off. *Ark.*" His squawk was embarrassed. "Goin' to take the old woman her voice back. See what you've done? Now *I'm* doin' good deeds! *Ark!* Nice to meet you 'n' all that. . . . Don't suppose we'll meet again." He spread his tattered wings and flew through the broken window.

As he disappeared, Queen Bluebell got to her feet, brushing down her skirt. "Horrid bird! What *was* he talking about? Now, Horace, old chap, don't know what's been goin' on here." She swayed and put her hands to her head. "Goodness! Feel a bit . . . a bit out of it. Up too early this morning, I expect. That'll be the reason! No doubt about it. Up too early, and I'm not as young as I was. But I've brought you a cook. Good lad. Name of Marshling. Determined type. Won't stand any nonsense from that daughter-in-law of yours."

There was an outraged squeal, and Fedora emerged from under the table, looking ruffled. Tertius followed, looking anxious. "Queen Bluebell!" Fedora snapped. "How . . . how dare you!"

If Bluebell was surprised, she didn't show it. "Now then, Fedora, I've known you since you were in diapers, so don't try taking that tone with me. What you need is some help, and I'm here to give it. Your mother's a fine woman, but she never did know how to control you girls."

Fedora, scarlet with rage, stamped her foot. "I DO know what I'm doing!" She waved *The Handbook of*

Palace Management under the queen's nose. "I've got this! I don't need any other help at ALL, thank you!"

The queen plucked the book from Fedora's hand and tossed it out the window with a grandiloquent gesture. "A load of old rubbish!"

"It's NOT!" Fedora was crying with anger.

"Actually, Your Highness, it is." Marshling Stonecrop had been standing in the doorway ever since Gubble had made his dramatic appearance, a wide-eyed Saturday and Bobby beside him. "My mum gave up working in a palace because of that book. She walked out. So did everyone else. Couldn't cope with all the rules and regulations."

Tertius put his arm around Fedora. "You're much too wonderful to need a stupid book, Feddy darling. Isn't she, Father?"

King Horace agreed with enthusiasm. "Absolutely! Splendid little thing! No need of any books!"

Fedora stood first on one leg, then on the other. "All right," she said at last. "Just as long as Marshling can make chocolate cake."

"It's what I'm best at," Marshling assured her. "Not so hot on the stew and potatoes just yet, but chocolate cake? I've won prizes."

Bluebell regarded her protégé with satisfaction.

"Good boy! Now, run down to the kitchen and make us all some tea."

Bobby put his hand up. "I'll make some toast!"

"Splendid idea, Bobby!" King Horace wiped his face with his handkerchief. "Just what we need."

"I'd better start cleaning up, like," Saturday volunteered.

Fedora looked down at the floor, then at Prince Tertius. "I'll . . . I'll give Saturday a hand," she said. "And . . . and if you want, Terty darling, you can ask all your old servants back."

King Horace gave a loud roar of approval. "Good girl! Tell you what. Give 'n' take 'n' all that. We'll get Mrs. Basket back to give young Marshling here a few tips, and then Mrs. B. can retire. She'd like that. Told me so herself. Is it a deal?"

Princess Fedora curtsied prettily to her father-in-law. "It's a deal," she said.

Chapter Twenty-six

Marcus and Gracie had already crept to a doorway. Now, quite unobserved, they slipped out and made their way to the outside world. Gubble stomped after them, Marlon on his shoulder acting as guide while Alf and Great-Uncle Alvin made helpful comments from above. Marcus was carrying one egg, Gracie the other. As they stepped into the yard, even the sunshine felt approving.

"I'll go and get the ponies," Marcus said. "You wait here," and he handed Gracie his egg.

Gubble sat down on the ground. "Ug," he said plaintively, rubbing at his head. "Poor Gubble. Nose in wrong place."

"Hmm." Gracie was looking thoughtful. "Gubble . . . can I try something?" Gubble did his best to nod, and Gracie carefully placed both eggs in his lap. Then she took hold of his ears and gave a sharp twist. "Phew! That's a relief. It worked!"

Gubble gazed at her, adoration in his eyes. "Nice. Much niceness. Good Gracie . . . Gracie Pillypot."

Gracie was still laughing as Marcus came back, leading Glee and Hinny. "What is it?" he asked.

"It's Gubble," Gracie explained. "He's happy because now his head's the right way around."

"That'll make it much easier for traveling," Marcus agreed. "Shall we get going?"

Gracie said nothing. She was looking up into the sky, and as Marcus followed her gaze, he caught his breath. Soaring high above the southern hills was a flight of dragons, their scales shining in the sunlight. Up and up they flew, then swooped, only to rise again. Marcus and Gracie watched in awe until at last the flight sank into the distant mists.

"Wow . . ." Marcus could hardly speak. He helped Gracie mount Hinny and waited while she wrapped the eggs in her cloak. "Do you think they know we're coming?"

"I'd say so," Gracie said. "I think they'll be waiting for us. They'll be on the other side of the southern border."

"And that's not far, Miss Gracie." Millie was suddenly hovering over Gracie's head. "I've been watching them all day. That golden dragon, Miss Gracie, she's been all of a twitch. Knew just what was happening, I'd say."

Gracie nodded. "I'm sure you're right, Millie. We'd better hurry."

With the aid of a convenient mounting block, Gubble was settled on Glee, and Marcus swung himself up behind him. "I'll show you the quickest way, Miss Gracie," Millie said, and the cavalcade set off.

There was little conversation as they made their way along the path. The dragons had left them with a strange sense of peacefulness, and as they drew nearer to the border, this feeling increased. Even Alf and Marlon were quiet; Great-Uncle Alvin dozed in the saddlebag, and Millie flew silently in front as their guide.

The border guards were also asleep, leaning against the wooden fence. Marcus raised an eyebrow but made no comment as he opened the gate to let Gracie ride through.

Gracie shook her head and slid off Hinny's back. "I think we should go on foot now," she whispered. "Don't ask me why. I just think we ought to. . . . It feels more polite, somehow. . . ."

Marcus understood at once. He helped Gubble

down and tied the ponies to the gatepost. Great-Uncle Alvin woke and stretched, and as Alf and Marlon flew to join Millie, Great-Uncle Alvin took up his perch on Gracie's shoulder. Gracie could feel him trembling but was unsure if it was with fear or excitement.

"Go on, Trueheart," he whispered. "Step forward!"

Then Marcus, Gracie, and Gubble walked out into the southern lands . . . and as they walked, they could feel the earth vibrating beneath their feet. There was a warm wind; as they went farther and farther, it grew warmer and warmer. A faint smell of smoke hung in the air. Emerging from under the trees, they saw a wide green meadow in front of them. Both Marcus and Gracie found themselves tiptoeing, and even Gubble did his best to walk softly on his flat green feet.

"Shh!" Gracie caught at Marcus's sleeve. "Can you hear it?"

Marcus could. It was the sound of beating wings, and the three stood still and waited.

"Here they come. Look, Trueheart, look! It's Lumiere . . ." Alvin gave a small, half-stifled sob. "Lumiere and Indigo and Luskentyre . . . I never thought I'd see them again."

★   ★   ★

Lumiere, the female dragon, was the first to arrive. Her eyes were liquid gold, and her scales glittered and shone. She bowed her head to Gracie as she landed on the springy green turf. "Trueheart," she said. "Trueheart." Behind her the blue and green dragons folded their gleaming wings as they, too, settled in the meadow; Indigo, his steel-gray eyes wide and watchful, gave only the slightest indication that there were humans present, but the sea-green shimmering Luskentyre lowered his heavy crested head in greeting.

Gracie's heart was hammering in her chest as she and Marcus walked forward and placed the eggs gently on a tussock of soft grass. "Please," Gracie said, "here they are." Marcus bowed, then stood very straight as if he were on guard.

As Lumiere drew closer, a thin crack appeared in first one egg and then the other. The dragon breathed softly over them, and her warm smoky breath made Gracie cough. Marcus's eyes were watering, but he remained at attention. There were more cracks, then a series of small squeaks and cries as two tiny dragons crawled out of the empty shells and half ran, half skittered toward their mother. She lifted her head and called, her voice as richly golden as her eyes and scales. The baby dragons stretched their wings and called back, their voices as high-pitched as the echo of a fine glass bell. And then they flew. They fluttered unsteadily at first, then with more confidence. They twirled and looped, then looped again for the sheer joy of it, and at last they flew to their mother. With enormous tenderness, she nuzzled them, before turning once again to Gracie and Marcus. "Truehearts," she said softly. "Truehearts . . ." Then, as the tiny dragons tucked themselves safely on their mother's back, Lumiere looked at Great-Uncle Alvin. "Old friend," she said, "will you come with us?" And Great-Uncle Alvin spread his ancient leathery wings.

"Unc? Unc! What are you doing?"

Alf's squeak was lost in the sound of rushing wind as Lumiere stretched her golden neck and soared into the air. As Indigo and Luskentyre rose with her, the nearby trees bent and shook as if blown by a gale, and leaves swirled and scattered across the bright green grass.

Gracie clutched Marcus's arm, and Alf sheltered under Gracie's cloak; Marlon rode the eddies and currents as best he could. Only Gubble remained solidly unmoved.

When all three dragons were skyborne, Lumiere made one last swoop and circled low above Marcus and Gracie. "Truehearts . . ." she called, and her golden voice rang loud. "Truehearts . . . farewell!"

★　★　★

There was silence in the meadow, and for a long while nobody moved or spoke. At last Gubble said, "Ug. Good. Gubble like." A subdued Alf squeaked agreement, then was quiet.

"Can't believe old Unc went off with them." Marlon shook his head. "I'll miss the old misery-guts. Hope he knew what he was doing."

Gracie smiled at him. "He looked happy. Very happy."

Millie sniffed and wiped her nose with her wing. "He was never happy here."

"The whole thing was . . ." Marcus shook his head. "*Amazing* doesn't even begin to cover it."

"I know." Gracie's eyes were bright with unshed tears. "Wasn't it truly and utterly and absolutely wonderful!" She suddenly laughed, swung around, and turned a cartwheel in the middle of the meadow. "I've just remembered something."

"What's that?" Marcus asked.

Gracie laughed again. "Today's my birthday! And we've seen a flight of dragons. . . . How perfect is that?"

"Ug." Gubble took Gracie's hand. "Happies, Gracie Pillypot. Much happies." And then, hopefully, he asked, "Cake?"

"I do hope so," Gracie said. "Let's go and see. . . ."

＊　＊　＊

In the House of the Ancient Crones, the Ancient One was putting the finishing touches on an enormous birthday cake. The Oldest One, holding a box of candles, asked, "Are you sure she'll be home today?"

Edna gave her companion a sharp look. "Of course she will. Didn't you see the web? Smooth as silk. She's dealt with whatever the unpleasantness was, and dealt with it for good. There's not a sign of it left. An excellent result."

Professor Scallio—comfortably settled in the largest chair in the kitchen with a cup of tea in one hand and a piece of toast in the other—nodded. "It certainly looks like it. A great relief, I must admit."

Elsie pulled off her wig and scratched her bald head. "I was thinking Gracie might prefer to celebrate with Marcus."

"On their own?" Edna shook her head. "She'll want to be here with us."

"We'll see." Elsie carefully replaced her red curls. "But she's growing up."

The Ancient One nodded. "And quite right, too, Elsie. But she's not growing up *that* fast. Tell you what . . . you set a place for Marcus, and I'll send the path to fetch them home."

"Wheeee!" Alf was twirling in ecstatic circles. "Look, Uncle Marlon! *Look!* The path's come to meet us 'n' we're going to go home 'n' we're going to have a PARTY!"

Marlon was inspecting the path, which was quivering hopefully at the edge of the meadow. It gave an encouraging ripple — but Marlon looked doubtful. "Hmm. Gets me dizzy, traveling on that."

"Oh, Dad." Millie sighed loudly. "Don't be such an old grouch. You sound just like Great-Uncle Alvin."

Marlon zigzagged over Marcus's head and onto Gracie's shoulder. "Never let it be said that I sound like Unc. All the best for today, kiddo. Let's go party!"

Alf looped a double-spiral backflip of his own invention that bore a very faint resemblance to the shape of a heart. "Have you wished her a happy birthday, Mr. Prince? Have you?"

Marcus grinned. "Not yet," and he leaned forward and kissed Gracie on the cheek. "Happy birthday, Gracie Gillypot."